'I want to talk a [...]
'About getting m [...]

Mallory smoothed down [...] [...]
blanket. It was so soft and comforting. She wanted
to wrap it around herself and block out this
conversation. But they'd been hiding from the
truth for too long now.

'How can we talk about getting married, when we
can't even look each other in the eye any more?'

He glanced away, proving her point.

See? she wanted to say. But she didn't. It hurt
too much.

How had it happened? They'd been best friends
for so many years. She didn't regret that they'd had
a child—how could she be sorry she had Angel? If
only she hadn't complicated matters by falling in
love with him.

'You're right,' Drew said. 'Things have been
different between us. But we can get married and
work out our problems.'

'Why are you arguing for something you obviously
don't want?' Not since Angel was born had he
looked at her with the passion he'd once been
barely able to contain.

Yet, it wasn't just the baby's birth that had cooled his
ardour, Mallory knew. She'd made the mistake of
crossing the line. She'd gone from friend to lover.

And soon she would be the same as all his other
lovers. History.

Dear Reader,

Welcome to the emotional world of Superromance™!

This month we have the first in a special set of themed novels we are going to be offering you throughout the year. *Her Best Friend's Baby* by CJ Carmichael is the first of the NINE MONTHS LATER novels, centring on pregnancy and that exciting time before the baby arrives...

Muriel Jensen (*The Third Wise Man*) and Janice Kay Johnson (*The Baby and the Badge*) continue their fabulous family sagas, and it won't be long until you see these wonderful writers back again. Janice will finish her trilogy in March and Muriel is going to return in June, with a great NINE MONTHS LATER book.

SEAL It With a Kiss by Rogenna Brewer is very different and refreshing; it's the kind of book that shows you how exciting Superromance can be. Not many women would want to be a Navy SEAL, but Tabitha Chapel is an extraordinary woman who's about to take on an extraordinary man! And there's a follow-up book coming in April, so enjoy!

All the best,

The Editors

Her Best Friend's Baby

CJ CARMICHAEL

SILHOUETTE
SUPERROMANCE

First published in Great Britain 2002
Silhouette Books, Eton House, 18-24 Paradise Road,
Richmond, Surrey TW9 1SR

© Carla Daum 2000

ISBN 0 373 70891 2

38-0102

Printed and bound in Spain
by Litografía Rosés S.A., Barcelona

Dear Reader,

Don't you love the friends you've had practically all your life? Isn't there an extra intimacy, a greater comfort zone?

That's what I've found, and it's also the case with Mallory, Drew, Grady and Claire. These four friends grew up together in the charming resort town of Port Carling, Ontario. Located north of Toronto, in Muskoka lake country, it has one of the most beautiful settings imaginable. Close your eyes and picture a clear blue lake surrounded by majestic pines. There, you've got Port Carling!

These four friends are very close, and yet they have secrets. About harmless mistakes in some instances, about serious ones—those with the potential to damage lives—in others.

Her Best Friend's Baby is Mallory and Drew's story. It's about a friendship that began when they were both in nappies, and an indiscretion that changed their friendship forever.

After you finish reading about them, I hope you'll look for *The Fourth Child*, my next Superromance™ book, due to be published in April, about Claire, who's been married for twelve years but who's never managed to forget the love of her life. You'll also find out what happens to Grady, and how he manages to turn his life around after—

Well, that would be telling!

Sincerely,

CJ Carmichael

For best friends everywhere, including mine: Myrna, Rhonda, Simon, Voula. And most of all, Michael.

ACKNOWLEDGEMENT

Thanks to Mary Jane, Chris and the rest of the staff at the *Olds Gazette*.

CHAPTER ONE

JUST GOES TO SHOW, you never can tell. Mallory
Lombard leaned against her bathroom counter and
stared at the strip from the pregnancy kit.

The old saying had been one of her aunt Norma's
favorites. Mallory had heard it often, usually when
her aunt was feeling sorry for herself and the way
her life had turned out.

Aunt Norma's dream had been to teach English
in the Far East. But in her last year of university,
her sister and brother-in-law were killed in a car
crash driving home to Port Carling from Toronto
after an anniversary celebration.

They both died instantly, at twelve minutes past
one on that warm evening in May. And at that moment Aunt Norma inherited a lovely old house in
Port Carling, a large insurance settlement and the
responsibility for raising her five-year-old niece,
Mallory.

So much for the teaching contract in Japan, a contract she'd received only that week. *Just goes to
show...*

Mallory kept staring at the strip in her hands,

hands usually steady enough to thread a needle in one try. According to the test's directions, the extra gray stripe on the small wand meant she was pregnant. And according to the box, the test was ninety-nine percent accurate.

How funny that only months earlier, on her thirty-fifth birthday, she'd resigned herself to a future without a husband or children. Time to face the truth, she'd told herself. Every one of her romantic relationships had been a disaster of one sort or another. Even she had realized that her current boyfriend was not good husband or father material.

Yet here she was, only six months later. Pregnant.

Mallory put the strip down on the counter and went to the kitchen to make coffee. No, wait. If she was pregnant, shouldn't she avoid caffeine? She scrounged her cupboards and found some peppermint tea.

As she waited for the water to boil, she wondered what other women in her situation would be feeling right now. Disbelief? Panic? Fear?

Yet she felt none of the above. Only calm acceptance. And, yes—a pinprick of excitement.

Okay, so the situation wasn't ideal. She wasn't married and the father would doubtlessly be dismayed at the news. But she wanted this baby....

Mallory thought about one of the newborn sleepers she'd unpacked from the fall shipment she'd received last week for her boutique. The soft turquoise cotton outfit had looked so tiny hanging on the white plastic hanger. For some reason she'd paused to stick her hand inside the fuzzy interior. The feet were the size of her thumbs.

This will never sell. It's much too small. I should have ordered the three-month size. Maybe even the six, she'd paused, fingering the white-and-yellow embroidered bears that danced along the neckline and the cuffs of each sleeve. Adorable.

She'd put the sleeper on display, but as she'd suspected, it hadn't sold. It was still hanging there now, just waiting for the perfect buyer to come along.

Just goes to show, you never can tell.

SIX WEEKS LATER, MALLORY was drinking herbal tea at Claire Ridgeway's cottage and munching on Claire's homemade macadamia-nut, chocolate-chip cookies.

She hadn't told anyone about her pregnancy yet, but now that she'd entered her twelfth week it was time. It made sense that Claire should be the first to know. They'd spent their summers together since they were small. Off the dock of Claire's parents' cottage on Lake Rosseau, they'd learned to swim, then water-ski.

In their teens they'd gone for ice cream at Steamboat Bay in Port Carling, often meeting Grady Hogan and, of course, Drew Driscoll, Mallory's next-door neighbor and best friend.

The four of them had hung out together for years, and even after graduation the ties had remained strong. Claire and her family spent many weekends and almost the entire summer at the cottage, and Grady had opened a custom boat manufacturing business in Port Carling and married his teenage sweetheart, Bess.

Drew was the only one who'd lost no time leaving Port Carling behind. Thinking of Drew and his high-powered journalism career reminded Mallory of her baby and the news she had yet to tell Claire.

"You look funny," Claire said, tilting her head so her chin-length blond hair touched one of her shoulders.

Hoarding her secret for a few more precious moments, Mallory asked, "Where are Kirk and the girls?"

"They've gone to town to get some groceries and the *Globe*. You know Kirk. He hates to be unplugged from the business world for even a weekend." Claire reached for a cookie. "I shouldn't be doing this," she said before taking a nibble.

"Give me a break, Claire. You have a knockout figure and you know it." Even with the few extra pounds Claire had gained after having children, she still turned heads in her bathing suit.

"I'd rather have your athletic build."

"Oh, sure." Mallory didn't believe her for a minute, but the argument was an old one between them.

She bit into her cookie, then remembered her baby and smiled.

"You have something to tell me, don't you?" Claire asked. "Look at that grin! Must be good news."

Mallory pressed her lips together to contain her excitement, but there was no holding back the joy that had built in the weeks since she'd realized she was pregnant. Now she could feel her eyes shimmer with moisture, and her mouth insisted on stretching like a rubber band.

"Mallory, you have to tell me. I'm dying of suspense. I knew something was up after you insisted on dropping in to say hello, even though you have to open your store in less than an hour."

Mallory glanced at her watch. Claire was right. She had to leave soon. She couldn't prolong the moment any longer.

"I'm pregnant."

Claire's mug landed with a thud on the kitchen's granite countertop. "What?" She looked as if she'd heard all right but couldn't believe the words.

"I'm going to have a baby, Claire." Mallory wrapped her arms around herself; it was all she could do to keep from dancing around the room with happiness.

Slowly, understanding—and pleasure—rounded out Claire's sapphire eyes. "A baby… Oh, Mallory…" She slid off her stool and engulfed Mallory in a hug. Pulling back, she gave her a searching look. "You're happy? It wasn't an ac—"

"Maybe a little." A little? Try totally. "But I am happy. You know how much I adore children." She loved Claire's three girls and Grady's twin boys almost as if they were her own.

Had Claire or Grady ever suspected a painful jealousy knotted her affection? Especially now that Claire had had her third child. *Third.* Sometimes Mallory wondered if her friend had any idea how lucky she was.

"And the father? Randall?"

"Claire, you sound like you're talking about an infectious disease every time you say his name. No, the baby isn't Randall's. I have more sense than that."

"I'm glad. He was too wrapped up in his old life to start a new one." Claire paused. The look she gave Mallory was definitely expectant.

Avoiding Claire's questioning gaze, Mallory ran her palms across her tummy. It was still depressingly flat, although there was a noticeable fullness to her breasts, which tingled at the slightest touch. She could barely wait for the day she'd need to go shopping for maternity clothing; she yearned to feel the bulk of her baby under her hands.

Claire froze as an idea came to her. "You didn't go to a sperm bank, did you?"

Mallory laughed. "Claire, you get the funniest

ideas. No, I didn't, but I can't tell you who the father is. At least not yet.''

She had to tell Drew first. Something she should have done weeks ago, when she'd first found out. But somehow she always had a good reason for not phoning....

Claire's eyes narrowed. ''It's not like you to be so mysterious.''

Mallory just shrugged. True, she didn't often keep secrets from Claire. But this was a special circumstance.

''I remember when Jenna was born you said if you weren't married by the time you were thirty-five, you might take matters into your own hands, but I never dreamed you meant it.''

Then Claire laughed. ''Oh, this is so exciting.'' She grasped Mallory's hands. ''I've still got Jenna's baby clothes, if it's a girl. And the crib and high chair...'' She paused, her expression becoming serious. ''But doing this on your own. Are you sure?''

''I've never felt so right about anything in my life. When I think there's a baby growing inside me right now—nothing else matters.''

''I'm glad for you, Mallory. I really am. I just hope you've thought this through. The idea of having my girls without Kirk...''

Claire was acting as if Mallory had planned the pregnancy. But Mallory didn't correct her. ''You have three children—I'm only going to have one.

And I may not have a man, but I have my friends."
Mallory had already made up her mind she wouldn't
count on any help from Drew. This was her baby,
her decision.

"I can't argue with you there. And frankly, at
times it feels like Kirk's only role in this family is
bringing home the paycheck."

"Financially, I'm more than prepared. My business is doing well, and I have that inheritance from
my parents." Her aunt Norma had used a portion of
it to raise her, but a significant amount of money
had remained when Mallory turned twenty-one and
the trust passed to her control.

She could have gone away to school, but she was
a homebody. So she'd invested some of the inheritance in her own business and socked the rest away
in reputable mutual funds. When her baby was born,
she intended to set up a trust fund to ensure her
child's future.

"And why shouldn't your business be doing
well? You have the prettiest store in Steamboat
Bay."

Steamboat Bay. The name had captured Mallory's
imagination as far back as she could remember. She
loved the fact that many of her customers arrived by
boat and parked at the docks in front of the lakeside
stores.

Claire squeezed Mallory's hands again. "I still
can't believe it's true. When are you going to tell

the others? Wouldn't it be fun to make an announcement at Thanksgiving dinner?''

Traditionally, the Thanksgiving long weekend, the second in October, marked the end of cottage season in the Muskokas, and Claire and Kirk usually hosted an end-of-the-season feast for their friends.

Mallory snapped her fingers. ''That reminds me. Did you think of inviting Drew's mother? With Drew out of the country again, Angie'll be alone.''

This would be one of the few times Drew hadn't made it home for the holiday. He'd phoned Angie a few weeks ago, and Angie had passed the message on to Mallory that he'd accepted an assignment in Tel Aviv.

Typical Drew. He was Mallory's closest friend, but even she didn't understand what motivated him to work so hard and pursue each new story with such unwavering enthusiasm. It was more than plain ambition. Drew's restless nature had never let him stay still for long. He thrived on a life-style that put him in Washington one minute, Ukraine the next.

That restlessness also applied to his love life. He changed girlfriends almost as frequently as he changed assignments. Occasionally, he brought a woman home for one of the holidays—but never the same one twice. Gorgeous, sophisticated women whom Mallory found slightly intimidating. She was always happier when he arrived alone.

"I phoned this morning, but Angie must have been working at the *Gazette*," Claire said.

"Actually, she went to Toronto to visit some friends. Should be back sometime this morning. Did you leave a message?"

"Yes, so hopefully, she'll be able to come."

"That's great. I'm going to pick up a pumpkin on my way to the store. Do you think three pies will be enough?"

A commotion at the front door distracted Mallory from Claire's answer. Kirk and the girls were back from town. The girls scrambled through the door and ran to give Mallory a big hug.

"Andie, Daisy, Jenna, it's so good to see you!" She wrapped her arms around all three. "What did you find in town?"

"Bad news." This was from Kirk, who was removing his hiking boots at the front door, leaning against the back of a pine bench for balance. Kirk had medium-brown hair, tanned skin and a fit body that bespoke his love of swimming. His gray wire-rimmed glasses gave him the serious business look that suited his profession as a stockbroker.

"What?" Claire's eyes sharpened on her husband. "Girls, can you carry those packages to the kitchen. Help yourselves to Popsicles once everything's put away."

"Angie Driscoll," Kirk said. "Didn't I hear you talking about her when I came in?"

"Yes," Mallory said, trying not to be impatient. Kirk had the worst habit of releasing information in trickles. And it didn't help to hurry him.

"I ran into Buddy Conroy when I was getting the groceries. He'd just had a call from Toronto General Hospital."

Mallory glanced at Claire and saw her own fear reflected in her friend's eyes. "Hospital?"

"Apparently, Angie was visiting friends in Toronto."

Mallory and Claire nodded impatiently.

"Last night she collapsed in the lobby of her hotel and was rushed to the General."

"What was wrong?" Claire placed a hand on her husband's shoulder.

"From what I hear it was complications from cancer."

Cancer. Mallory's insides lurched.

"No one knows where the cancer started, but it spread rapidly. She died last night."

Died. Mallory sank onto the sofa, vaguely aware of Claire dropping her head on her husband's chest.

"Poor Angie," Claire said softly. "Was anyone with her?"

Kirk shook his head. "Her friends thought she was resting in her room with a headache. And no one in Port Carling even realized she was sick. According to Buddy, she hadn't told a soul about being ill."

Mallory couldn't say anything. She was in shock. All her life she'd lived next door to Angie Driscoll. How could the older woman have been so sick without Mallory knowing? Okay, Angie had started to slow down a little, but Mallory had attributed that to age. No normal person could cope with Angie's hectic schedule in their youth, let alone their late fifties.

Those trips to Toronto had grown more frequent lately, but Mallory had just thought Angie was getting a little restless. She'd even wondered if the older woman might have found herself a beau. It hadn't occurred to her that the trips might be medical in nature.

"Are you okay, Mallory?" Claire put a hand to her friend's forehead. "I know you and Angie were close."

Yes. Angie had been like a mother. Aunt Norma had fed and clothed Mallory, but Angie was the one who'd welcomed her with a smile, who'd never been too busy to stop her work and chat. Mallory had spent a lot of hours at the Driscoll house. Not just because of Angie, of course, but because of Drew....

Drew. Mallory's throat closed at the thought of her oldest and closest friend. He couldn't have known how sick his mother was or he would never have canceled his trip home for Thanksgiving, no matter how big the story he was covering.

Would he? Mallory quickly cast aside the momentary doubt.

Angie meant the world to Drew. If he'd known about the cancer, he certainly hadn't known how serious it was.

"ARE THESE YOUR PLANE TICKETS?" The attractive blonde picked up a package lying on Drew Driscoll's desk. She'd already folded a couple of his cotton shirts and a clean pair of chinos for his suitcase.

"Thanks, Trish. You're a peach for helping me pack for Tel Aviv like this. Sorry there isn't time to take you out to brunch."

Last night they'd gone for dinner, then ended up on the pullout couch in his office. They'd met coincidentally on a plane from Winnipeg to Ottawa late that afternoon; they hadn't seen each other in years.

This time he'd been returning from researching a story on the current foreign affairs minister, while Trish was on her way to a four-day conference on Implementing Change in the Year 2000. She'd missed last evening's welcome dinner, and now she was rushing to make the first morning work session.

"Want me to give you a ride to the airport?" Trish offered. Her rental car was sitting in his monthly parking stall underneath the building.

"Why don't I grab a cab and save you the effort."

"It's no problem." She leaned over to kiss him lightly, then reached up to brush back his coarse dark hair.

"Drew, why doesn't your hair lie flat? It reminds me of the bristles on a paintbrush."

Drew finger-combed the top of his head.

"If you'd seen some of the things I've seen in this world, your hair would stand on end, too."

"Maybe you should tell me about them sometime."

"Maybe I should." He smiled, but as he picked up his bags, he was really thinking, *And maybe I shouldn't...* "Right now, though, I have a plane to catch. Are you sure you don't mind giving me a ride?"

"Not at all. It's on the way, more or less."

She smiled, but her eyes weren't in it. Probably she was thinking about her conference, just as he was thinking about his work. They'd had fun together, but it was time to move on.

He was following her out the door, when he heard the phone ring.

"Forget it," Trish advised. "You're already late. Let your machine answer.

He paused momentarily, then shook his head. "It'll just take a sec." Dashing back, he picked up on the fifth ring.

"Driscoll here."

The voice on the other end of the line was unfamiliar. The woman gave her name and that of a hospital in Toronto, but none of the information penetrated.

"Am I speaking with Andrew Driscoll?"

"Yes."

"The son of Angela Driscoll from Port Carling, Ontario?"

"Yes," he said again, sinking into a chair.

"I'm sorry, but I have bad news, sir. Your mother passed away at our hospital a few hours ago."

Drew swallowed and struggled to take in the news. Angie dead? But how? Why?

"An accident?" he tried to ask, but his voice gave out on him. He cleared his throat. "Was she in a car accident?"

"No, sir. She was in Toronto for a medical appointment and to visit some friends. She collapsed and was rushed by ambulance to the hospital. We did everything we could, sir. Unfortunately, the cancer had spread too far...."

Cancer? God, he'd had no idea. Had Angie? Surely not, because if she had, then she'd have told him. He brushed his hands over his face and tried to concentrate on what he was being told.

"I'm sorry we couldn't reach you earlier. We had some difficulty tracking down your office number."

He cursed the fates that he hadn't gone home last

night. He'd planned to, but then he'd met Trish, and decided it really wasn't necessary since he kept a stash of clothing at his office for just this purpose.

"Are you okay, sir? Is someone with you?"

"Yeah, someone is with me." He thought about his friends in Port Carling, Mallory in particular. She'd lived next door to Angie all her life. They'd been so close. Had she heard? He'd phone her on his cell phone en route to the airport. God, he couldn't wait to see her.

"Drew?" Trish had backtracked into his office. "We're late."

He quickly thanked the hospital nurse and set down the receiver. "Change of destination."

"What happened?"

"My mother's died. I've got to go home."

CHAPTER TWO

HIS MOTHER COULDN'T BE DEAD. There *had* to be some mistake. He'd talked to her two weeks ago.

Guilt cut into the numb emptiness in Drew's gut. He should have phoned more often. He should have gone home more often. Hell, there were a lot of things he should have done more often.

He thought back to their short five-minute conversation. He'd had no hint that she wasn't feeling well. She'd been mulching down the raspberries for the winter when he'd called.

He had such a clear picture of her at the task. Wearing her old gardening togs, that straw hat he'd brought her from Mexico City. He could see her booted foot on the spade, the suede gardening gloves she always wore....

No. That she was gone just wasn't possible. People so sick they were about to die didn't mulch down gardens, publish weekly newspapers and talk to their sons as though nothing were wrong.

Maybe there'd been a mistake with the identification. Maybe it was another Angela Driscoll.

Drew stared out the small window of the 767, into

the pale-blue void. Was he really hurtling at five hundred miles an hour through space, thirty-odd thousand feet from the earth? Nothing seemed real to him, not even his hand, which was resting on the pullout tray, holding tight to the glass of scotch he'd just ordered.

The lines on his knuckles were deeper than he remembered; the dark color of his skin seemed more weathered than tanned. That wasn't the hand of a young man anymore.

Thirty-five years old.

When had it happened? How had it happened?

It felt like only months since he'd sat at the kitchen table, working on math problems while his mother puzzled over her weekly editorial.

"Those jet skis are getting completely out of control," she'd mutter, while he worried about memorizing geometry theorems.

Oh, Angie. Angie…

At some point he'd started calling her by her given name. She'd smiled the first time, but she hadn't objected.

Mother. Mom.

Why wouldn't she have told him she had cancer? How long had she known? Had she suffered terribly? He should've been warned how little time they had left together. He could have gone home for a while, helped ease some of the demands in her life.

Really? Which stories would you have dropped to

find the time? He pushed self-doubt aside. He would have done what he had to do. Like now. He thought about the flight he should have been taking—to Heathrow Airport, where he would have connected with El Al to Tel Aviv.

He felt a moment's regret for the story that was now out of his hands. He couldn't deny it hurt to give it up. But for his mother he would have given up more.

Oh, God, it wasn't fair. There was so much they hadn't talked about. Her past, her childhood, even his grandparents. He was amazed now at how little he knew. How his family had ended up in Port Carling. What it had been like running the newspaper when Angie was young, when her grandfather was just starting up.

About his mother's personal life. On that topic he was almost completely ignorant. What was the grand passion his grandpa had occasionally hinted at that had ended when she'd left Port Carling to go to journalism school in Toronto? And why hadn't she ever married? As a child, it had seemed natural to him that he should be the center of her universe. Only recently had he begun to wonder why she'd chosen to live the way she had.

Could it have been because of his father? The man who'd been responsible for his conception but who'd never been a part of his life? Maybe he'd hurt Angie so bad she'd never recovered.

Drew clenched his hand. That was another topic he and Angie had never talked about. Why hadn't he been more curious about his father?

He remembered the first time the topic had come up, around Father's Day when he was in kindergarten and all the other kids were making pencil holders out of Popsicle sticks for their dads. The teacher had pulled him aside and suggested he make one for his grandpa.

At home that night he'd asked his mother why he didn't have a dad like the other kids.

"There isn't a lot I can tell you, Drew. I'm sorry, but I don't even have a picture. I know it's hard. I expect you'll just have to learn to accept it, though."

When he was around eleven or twelve, she'd told him more. "I was in my last year of journalism at Ryerson when I got pregnant. There was a journalist from the States. We dated a couple of times while he was in town working on a story. His name was David. I know it seems ridiculous, but I can't remember his last name. We only saw each other a few times, and of course I hadn't *planned* on having a baby...."

Funny how he'd never questioned that story of hers. Now his investigative mind saw the flaws. Sexual attitudes when his mother was growing up were quite different from current ones. Would his mother have slept with a man she'd seen just a few times? And had she really forgotten his last name?

Yet what good would asking questions do him? The one person who could answer them was gone.

If he'd known she was sick, if he'd gone back to Port Carling to look after her, maybe he could have found out some of the answers. Now it was too late.

She was gone and he could hardly stand to think of the void that would leave in his life.

He downed his scotch in one swallow, then settled his forehead against his hand. With his index finger he wiped away a tear, then another. He supposed a guy was entitled to feel sorry for himself at a time like this. But it wasn't true that he was alone.

He thought about his friends. Grady, who shared his passion for waterskiing, fishing and hockey. Claire, who mothered him in ways Angie hadn't, bringing him home-baked treats when she came to visit, offering to hem his pants or sew on a button when he was looking particularly bedraggled.

And finally, Mallory, who only seemed to notice the good in him, no matter what he did. Not just in him, to be fair. He remembered his mother saying, "She sees the world through rose-colored glasses. And the world *would* be rose colored—if there were more people like Mallory in it."

He'd called her from the car on his way to the airport. She'd insisted on picking him up at Pearson International in Toronto, even though he could easily have rented a car, which he usually did on his visits home.

"No sense in that," Mallory had said. "You can use your mom's Explorer once you get to Port Carling."

Drew considered the unspoken context. Because Angie wouldn't be using it anymore, would she? *Dead people don't drive.* It sounded like the title to a gruesome children's novel, the kind Claire and Kirk's eldest daughter, Andie, couldn't get enough of.

Dead people.

No. Not Angie. Angie wasn't "dead people." Angie was alive, with her husky laugh and her darting blue eyes that took in everything around her. Angie was full of energy, raising a child on her own, keeping up the huge vegetable and perennial gardens her mother had tended all her life and publishing the *Hub of the Lakes Gazette* every week.

A series of high-pitched beeps sounded in the airplane cabin. The overhead lights flashed a warning for him to put on his seat belt.

Drew flipped his tray into the upright position.

Please let Mallory be waiting when he landed. He wanted so much to see her. Sweet-hearted, dependable Mallory.

He thought about their last visit, when she'd come to his cottage in the Gatineaus for a weekend of hiking in July. They'd been alone together so many times he couldn't count. Yet that last occasion had been different. Why had he reached out to stroke her face when they were sitting by the fire drinking wine and complaining about the weather? And why had she caught his hand and held it there?

God, he still couldn't believe they'd actually made love. Twice that day and once the next morning before she left. It had felt so right. That was the truly amazing part.

But it had been a mistake. Lovers came and went; friends like Mallory were forever. Sex didn't belong in their relationship, even if it was absolutely the best he'd ever had.

This would be the first time they'd seen each other since that weekend, and he felt uneasy. Would everything be the same between them?

It would. Mallory had promised. Things could have been so awkward when they'd said their good-byes after that weekend, but she'd kissed him lightly on the cheek the way she usually did and told him not to worry. "We shouldn't have," she'd said, "but it was fun."

Yes, it was. And maybe it had been bound to happen. Once.

"Still friends for life?" he'd asked when he'd dropped her off at the airport.

"Yes," she'd promised. And Mallory always kept her word.

THERE SHE WAS, watching suitcases as they shot down the chute and landed with a thud on the rotating luggage carousel. Drew picked up his pace, feeling the corners of his mouth pull up into his first smile since he'd received the phone call about his mother.

Mallory was wearing a muted-green wool sweater and tan corduroy pants. The scarf twisted around her throat added the colors of the autumn leaves—red and gold—to her outfit. Her thick mop of curly light-brown hair was pulled back in her usual ponytail, and even from yards away he could see the dusting of freckles that highlighted her nose and upper cheeks.

"Hey!" he called out, feigning anger, "does that suitcase belong to you?"

She'd picked his worn leather bag off the conveyor belt and was hoisting it onto the floor beside her. At his words she swung a guilty-looking face in his direction, then shook her head when she saw who it was.

"As if anyone would want to steal your decrepit-luggage. Don't you get paid, now that you're working freelance?"

He wrapped his arms around her and swung all five feet eight inches of her off the floor. She squeezed him tight, not letting go when he settled her back on the ground. Her hair, smelling of herbs and sunshine, brushed up against his cheek and under his nose; its rough texture made him want to sneeze.

"Don't you use conditioner?" he complained, pushing a strand away from his eyes.

"Don't you?" she countered, rubbing a hand over the top of his head.

Their eyes met, and the words he'd been planning to say next drained out of him. Sympathy, understanding and compassion were reflected in the deep pools of her green eyes. The pain that had gripped his chest suddenly loosened into something less like agony and more like simple sadness. She put a hand to his cheek and he held it there for a few minutes, watching as her eyes began to glitter with unshed tears.

Of all the people in the world, Mallory was the person who best understood what Angie had meant to him.

"I'm sorry, Drew. Angie was the best. The absolute best."

The last time he'd held Mallory was after they'd made love. But he wouldn't think about that now. Instead, he just lowered his arms and smiled, feeling a trace of regret.

He'd liked it better when he could hug her without remembering how perfect her small, upright breasts had appeared in the glow from the burning logs in his fireplace. Or how smooth her skin had felt under his lips as he'd trailed kisses over her entire body.

Amazingly, the loving hadn't felt awkward at the

time. After all, he'd been making love to a girl who'd seen him pee behind the raspberry bushes that divided his house from hers. Everything that long wild afternoon had felt so right.

Now he felt uncomfortable enough to make up for it.

"Don't, Drew." Mallory's hand was back on his face. Of course she knew what he was thinking, feeling. She always did. "What happened between us was beautiful. I don't want you to regret it."

"I don't," he said, but it was a lie. He pulled out a folding aluminum carrying frame on wheels and snapped it into position, then placed his leather bag on it with his briefcase on top. "Where did you park?"

"In the parking lot."

"Funny girl." He yanked her ponytail. "You lead, then."

When they'd found her dark-blue utility vehicle, he asked, "Can I drive?"

She unlocked the back and he loaded his luggage.

"Are you sure? You must be tired."

"Yeah. But I need to *do* something."

She tossed the keys in his direction. "Just remember which side of the road you're supposed to drive on, okay?"

Fingers groping the side of the driver's seat, he found the lever to move the seat back. "Mallory, you worry too much. I'm an excellent driver."

"Sure. And the last time you were here, when you turned into oncoming traffic?"

"I'd just spent six weeks in England. What could you expect?" He paid for the parking, ignoring the five-dollar bill she tried to press into his hand. Then he searched out the signs for Highway 401 east, which would take him to the 400.

Driving was good for him, requiring that he focus on simple matters of road signs, merging lanes and speed traps. Once they'd passed Canada's Wonderland, however, he had nothing to concentrate on but the occasional lane change, and his thoughts roamed.

"Where is...Mom?" he finally asked, avoiding the word *body*.

"At the funeral home in Bracebridge." Mallory's voice was soft, textured like velvet. "You know, of course, that Buddy Conroy was your mom's lawyer?"

He nodded. Buddy was the only lawyer in Port Carling, and a close family friend. Who else would Angie have used?

"Well, I spoke to Buddy briefly before I left to get you. He says they're waiting for instructions on the funeral. Angie didn't specify in her will what she wanted. It was a pretty old will, though. Made shortly after you were born, I think. Guess who your guardian is?"

"As long as it isn't your aunt Norma." He smiled

over the joke, but the picture of Angie's body stretched out in some dark wooden box made him want to start crying again.

He swallowed and pushed up the visor. The sun was low to his left now. "I've seen a few dead bodies in my line of work, but I've never had to make funeral arrangements before."

Mallory's gentle sigh wound itself around his heart. "I'm sure Angie would want to keep things fairly simple."

"Yeah."

They were both silent for a moment, then impulsively Mallory reached over to squeeze his shoulder. "It's so good to see you. If only—"

She didn't finish her sentence, but he knew what she meant. If only he were here for a different reason.

He stared at the cars in front of him, at the blue-gray asphalt that seemed to lead forever to the horizon. An optical illusion. The road had to end somewhere, didn't it? Right now he wished that it wouldn't. That he and Mallory could keep driving like this forever, and he would never have to face the reality of his mother's death, of the funeral and what would happen next....

"Did anyone know she was sick?" There. At last he'd asked the question that had plagued him from the moment he'd heard the news. "Because I sure as hell didn't."

"We wondered about that. But no, none of us knew, either. Maybe you can talk to her doctor about it. Or Buddy. She must have had a reason for not telling anyone."

"Maybe she was just too used to having nobody but herself to rely on." The idea was a bitter one, especially since it might have been true. Hadn't it been months since his last visit? But when he'd phoned to cancel out on Thanksgiving, no recrimination had tinged his mother's voice.

Yet guilt assailed him. If only he'd come as originally planned, on Thursday night, he would at least have been there for her last hours.

"Don't do this to yourself, Drew. Angie knew you loved her."

"Yeah." He swallowed. Somehow that didn't seem enough.

"Sure you wouldn't like me to drive?" Mallory asked.

Damn. He must have started crying again. He wiped at his eyes and shook his head. "I'm fine."

They drove awhile longer without talking, until a pedestrian overpass came into view ahead of them. "Do you want to stop at Weber's for a burger?" Mallory asked.

Food was the last thing he wanted, but Weber's was a tradition. "Of course." He pulled off the highway and parked in the lot on the right side of the road. Often, a long lineup of people flowed in and out of the fast-food restaurant, but the place wasn't that busy now. Most of the Thanksgiving traffic would have come through last night or earlier in the day.

They ordered chocolate shakes with their burgers and fries, and Drew had to admit that getting something in his stomach felt good. He noticed Mallory only ate a few bites, though, before she put down her food and slipped into the washroom.

When she came back she said she'd meet him in the car.

"Was it something I said?" he asked, settling in for the last two-thirds of the journey.

She tipped her head back on the headrest. "More like something I ate."

That didn't sound like the Mallory he knew. Usually, she ate like a horse. Well, healthy-sized portions, anyway. "Don't tell me you're developing a delicate constitution?"

Strangely, her cheeks flushed with color. What was going on? Why was she suddenly so sensitive?

Surely this wasn't because of the sex thing.

"Is everything okay?"

"Everything's fine. Really."

But she was staring out the passenger window, a hand pressed to her temple.

"Why don't you look at me when you say that?"

"Because you're supposed to be driving. Because…" Her voice faded. She turned her head and glanced at him. Took a deep breath, then smiled. It looked fake.

"Everything's okay. Really, Drew."

"'Cause if it's what happened the last time we saw each other..."

"Oh, Drew."

She sounded close to tears. Lord, that was it. He should have known better than to expect no aftermath. "Come on, Mallory. We gave in to urges we should have ignored. Can't we just forgive ourselves and move on?"

"I wish it were that easy."

"Why can't it be? Do you need someone to blame? Well, blame Grady, then. If he hadn't canceled out on us, we wouldn't have been alone, there wouldn't have been any opportunity..."

"That's true." Mallory sounded reflective. "Funny how little things in life can end up making such a big difference."

Drew bit back a retort. So they'd made love. It wasn't *such* a big deal, was it?

Dusk was falling. As he got back on the highway he reached for the knob that turned on the car's lights. The recently harvested farmland and acres of pasture dotted with dairy cattle had slowly given way to forest struggling for survival on the rocky Canadian Shield. Occasionally, Drew glimpsed the still waters of Lake Muskoka in the faded light.

"We're almost home now." He tried not to think

of how empty the house was going to be without Angie. Best to avoid that right now. Maybe he could stay with Mallory. Just this first night.

He glanced sideways and saw that her forehead was still set in a frown. Obviously, this wasn't the right time to ask. But they did need to talk. He couldn't take this tension between them.

Spotting a rest stop ahead, he put on his signal light. Once they were safely off the road, he shifted into neutral and turned off the ignition. Only then did he look at Mallory.

She'd twisted in her seat to face him, but her eyes were downcast. Her hands, he noticed, rested lightly against her stomach.

"Okay, Mal. If there's something we should discuss, let's get it out in the open."

"Yes." She nodded but still wouldn't look at him.

He reached out to take one of her hands. It felt cool and smooth and he rubbed his thumb over her pulse point.

"Mal, we can work this out. I know we can. Just speak to me, okay? You're making me nervous with this silent treatment. And *look* at me." With his other hand he reached for her chin and tilted her face upward.

"Drew, I'm sorry if I don't seem myself, but I don't want to talk. I can't stop thinking about Angie, and I'm sure you feel the same way. Let's get through the funeral, okay? Maybe then we can talk about…about what happened between us.''

She looked at him then, and her solemn gaze gave him a rumbling feeling in his chest. Oh, God. This was not going to be good.

Part of him protested, Why now? Why did Mallory have to start acting like such a damned woman now, when he needed her help to cope with Angie's death?

He knew his resentment was unjustified. She'd offered to put their issues behind them, at least until after the funeral.

"Okay, Mal. We'll do it your way. Let's go home.''

AT ELEVEN O'CLOCK they finally pulled into Port Carling. He drove up to the garage behind the house Mallory had lived in all her life, next door to his and Angie's.

"Do you want to stay at my place tonight?'' she asked. "It might be easier for you to go home in the morning.''

After the tension between them earlier, he was surprised at the offer. But glad for it, too.

"Yeah. Thanks, Mal.'' As he got out of the car, he found it hard not to remember the welcome Angie had always prepared for him when he visited. She'd have ready his favorite scotch and a collection of clippings she wanted to talk about. They'd stay up late, just chatting. Usually a few friends would drop in. And Mallory, of course. Always Mallory.

Angie's golden retriever, Doug, greeted them, barking and sniffing. Once they were inside, the dog glanced back at the door anxiously, as if waiting for someone else to arrive.

"I told Buddy I'd keep Doug until you got here," Mallory explained. "The poor guy hasn't left the door the whole time. He's waiting for Angie to pick him up."

Drew patted the animal's light-brown coat, then wiped his shoes on the bright cotton rug at the door. He set his bag on a bench shaped and painted to look like a cat, before glancing around.

The house was the same one Mallory had always lived in, but she'd made a lot of changes since Norma had left. Clutter for one. She had an aversion to empty space. Yet the net effect was not the mess you might expect.

Drew actually loved Mallory's place. It was warm and comfortable and there was always something interesting to feast your eyes on. Like this old creamery can filled with umbrellas. He was sure it hadn't been here last time he visited.

"I don't have any scotch. Would you like a beer?" She reached up to a cupboard filled with glasses of various shapes and sizes. All of them different colors. Mallory had something against matched sets, too; even her wooden kitchen chairs were each painted a different color.

"That'd be great." He went into the living room and turned on the television. Easing into the soft, worn leather of Mallory's sofa, he lifted his feet onto a nearby ottoman. A few moments later Mallory was beside him, handing him a glass of cold beer.

They watched the news without speaking, then stayed tuned as an old movie came on. *Butterflies Are Free*.

"I've always liked this movie," Mallory said. But ten minutes into it, she was asleep, her head on the armrest, her feet tucked up next to him to keep warm.

A cotton blanket had fallen to the floor. Drew picked it up and settled it over her. Her pale-brown eyelashes rested lightly on her still-flushed cheeks, and her apricot-colored lips were parted slightly with the relaxation of sleep. Somehow, the elastic holding her hair had worked its way loose, and her hair was a jumbled mass around her shoulders.

"What's happened, Mal?" he asked quietly. "Where's your stamina?" He couldn't count the number of times they'd stayed up late to see old, corny flicks. Usually, he conked out sooner than she did.

Ah, well. He refocused on the television, but the story fell flat now that he knew Mallory had dozed off. Maybe he ought to turn in, too. He switched off

the set, then put their glasses in the dishwasher.
Heaving his bag over his shoulder, he made for the
spare room, the room that used to be Norma's.

Mallory's aunt had left Port Carling shortly after
Mallory's high-school graduation. As far as Drew
knew, Mallory didn't mind much. She and Norma
had never been close.

Norma's old room now sat stripped of any sign
of her stern, cold personality. Mallory had painted
the walls a blue-green color and sewn a new duvet
and matching curtains. On the floor by the bed lay
one of those tied rag rugs Mallory was always working on, and favorite photographs she'd had blown
up and framed covered the walls.

Here was one of Drew and her when they were
young, sitting in a little inflated pool, blowing bub-
bles at each other. He had seen the photo often, but
now he stopped to examine it. They couldn't have
been more than five or six years old, he was sure.
And already they'd been the best of buds.

He smiled and brushed his index finger over the
glass that covered her small face. Then he hefted his
bag onto a hand-painted dresser.

Was he exhausted enough to sleep? He hoped so,
but just to be sure, he pulled out his vial of sleeping
tablets. Carrying his toilet bag, he went to brush his
teeth, careful to avoid the view from the window—
of the home he'd shared with his mother for more
than eighteen years.

When he was done, he popped his head around the corner. Mallory was still sleeping on the couch. Maybe he should carry her to her bed. But that would wake her for sure. Better to leave her as she was.

He grabbed another blanket from her bed and put it on top of the light cotton throw. She didn't budge. In fact, she hadn't moved an inch since he'd left her.

Obviously, she was exhausted. Yet she'd still picked him up at the airport, offered him a bed for the night.

Good old Mallory. He bent to kiss her forehead. *Sweet dreams, my friend.*

CHAPTER THREE

DREW AWOKE THE NEXT MORNING to the sound of running water and someone being sick.

He lifted his head from the pillow and heard it again. A retching, followed by the toilet flushing. The sounds were faint, almost muffled by the flow of water through the pipes, and the wall that separated his room from the bathroom.

But they were still unmistakable.

He stood and pulled on his jeans. Tapping on the bathroom door, he asked, "Mallory? Are you okay in there?"

They hadn't had that much to drink last night, had they? He'd had only one beer. And Mallory had been drinking juice.

"I'm fine."

There was the noise of more water running, then the door opened. Mallory was still dressed in her outfit from the day before. With a towel, she was mopping her damp face.

"Sorry. Do you need the bathroom?"

"No." He realized suddenly how badly he had to

pee. "Well, yeah, I guess I do. But it sounded like you were sick in there."

She looked at him as though he'd sprouted an extra eyeball. "I was just doing some cleaning. Sorry if I disturbed you."

Cleaning. Right. Just what most people did when they rolled off the couch in the morning. But he didn't call her on it. If she didn't want to admit she was sick, that was her business.

He shuffled in as she walked out. "Do I have time for a shower?"

"Take all the time you want. We're not meeting Buddy until ten."

Oh, God. The beginning of the legalese that would accompany Angie's death. He dreaded it, but then wondered if dealing with practical matters wasn't the best way to survive the next few days.

After he'd washed, shaved and changed into clean clothes, he found Mallory sitting in the kitchen with a mug in her hand. She was wearing a pair of jeans and an ivory-colored sweater that she'd owned forever. Her face was pale, but her eyes were bright and she was smiling.

"I made some coffee and there's bread for toast."

"Great." He didn't feel like eating, but remembering how much better he'd felt after the burger last night, he slid two slices of bread into the toaster, then reached for a mug. The coffee he definitely needed.

"When is Claire having Thanksgiving dinner?"

"Tomorrow at four. It's earlier than usual because Kirk and the girls are driving back to Toronto afterward. Claire is staying a couple of extra days for the funeral."

Funeral. He was beginning to hate that word. It sounded dreary, morbid, oppressive. Nothing like Angie.

"Today's Sunday, right?" he raised his head in time to see Mallory nod. "Want some more coffee?" He filled his own cup, then went to top up hers. But she put her hand over the mug.

"No, thanks. I'm drinking tea."

"I thought you couldn't put two words together unless you'd had your morning coffee."

She looked down at the table, where she was tracing a pattern with her index finger. "I'm sort of on this new health-food kick."

"You are?" He reflected on her suggestion last night that they stop for burgers and milk shakes. If that was her idea of health food, then it was okay with him.

He needed his coffee, though; thank goodness she still stocked the good stuff. He took another sip. "What time should we leave for Buddy's office?"

Mallory stood to rinse her mug. "We don't have to go anywhere. Buddy's meeting us at the house. Your house."

"Oh." He moved over by the sink and looked

out the open window. He could see right through the parted curtains into his mother's kitchen, and was reminded of all the nights he and Mallory had made faces at each other as they'd stood washing dinner dishes.

"I have a spare key if you need it."

"That's okay." His fingers dug into the front left pocket of his jeans until he found the piece of hard metal. "I brought mine with me."

"Would you like a few minutes over there alone first?"

He shook his head. Maybe he was a coward, but it would be easier if Mallory came with him. After he finished his toast, he led the way out her side door, past the raspberry bushes. The reddened leaves were already drying and falling to the ground.

"Did you have a good crop this year?" he asked, avoiding the prickly branches as he took the short-cut through the hedge.

"I've got ten bags in the freezer." Mallory hesitated a moment before adding, "Angie probably has some in hers, too."

"Yeah." He pulled the key from his pocket, then paused, his attention caught by the flapping of white cotton on Angie's clothesline. Three T-shirts hung stiff and dry in the early-morning sun.

Mallory followed his gaze. "I'm sorry. I should have taken those down. I've hardly done a thing since we found out."

"It doesn't matter." He inserted the key and opened the door. The smell that meant home wafted out to greet him, tinged with the scent of something sweet. Apples, he realized, when he saw a row of glass jars, neatly labeled, sitting by the stove.

He picked one up and looked at Angie's neat printing: Applesauce, October 1999. His mother hadn't been much of a cook, but she'd made good preserves. As a final gesture, it seemed fitting.

Beside him Mallory blew into a tissue. But oddly enough, here in his mother's kitchen he didn't feel as badly as he had earlier. Maybe because she hadn't been gone long and her presence still filled the air, along with the smell of apples and cinnamon.

He wandered around the rooms while Mallory put on another pot of coffee.

"Buddy will want some," she explained.

"Sure." He didn't care one way or the other. He had the strange feeling that his mother might show up any second. He could imagine her coming out from the bathroom, her hair wet from the shower. Or maybe he'd hear her step on the basement stairs as she returned from storing a batch of preserves in the cellar.

Pausing in the living room, he noted newspapers carefully stacked by the fireplace, and a wilted flower arrangement in the adjoining dining room.

Down the hall was the bathroom, floor clean, sink shining. He pulled aside the vinyl shower curtain and saw only the gleaming almond-colored tiles and chrome showerhead.

His room was as he'd left it in July, but without the dust that usually accumulated between visits. The last door was Angie's bedroom, and he paused before opening it.

If she'd left any secrets behind, here was where he'd find them. Had his mother been the type to collect memorabilia? He didn't even know. At some point he would have to go through all her things.

But later. For now he was the observer, on the outside looking in. And even here, in this room where Angie had been prone to pile dirty clothes until she'd run out of anything to wear, he found everything clean and organized.

All highly unusual. Angie must have tidied up before her trip to Toronto.

Maybe it had occurred to his mother that she might not return from her trip. Maybe that was why she'd left the house so spotless—

A knock sounded at the side door, and he made his way back to the kitchen.

By the time he'd walked down the short hall, Buddy Conroy was standing by the table, talking to Mallory. An inch or two over six foot, he was a powerfully built man, with steel-gray hair and light-blue eyes that Mallory always said were too pretty for a man. But then, she'd always said that about Drew's darker blue eyes, too.

"Drew. I'm sorry." Buddy's words were sincere, and he gripped Drew's hand in his.

"Thanks, Buddy. It sure was sudden. Do you know what happened?"

Mallory passed out mugs, which Drew filled from the French-press coffeemaker Angie had used for years. They seated themselves around Angie's old oak table, automatically leaving the chair she'd always sat in empty. Buddy stared at the vacant spot for a few seconds before answering.

"I talked to her doctor. Angie started getting headaches early this spring. By June they confirmed the diagnosis—inoperable brain tumor. Doctors told her she'd probably have a year, maybe a little less, but that she should get her affairs together as soon as possible."

June. So she'd known she was ill when he was here on vacation over the July long weekend. "Any idea why she didn't tell anyone?" Didn't tell *me?*

Buddy shook his head slowly. "Angie didn't want anyone feeling sorry for her. Or that was what she told her doctor. Maybe she was in denial. She never did do anything about her affairs. This will—" he pulled a sheaf of papers from the manila folder he'd been carrying "—is at least thirty years old. She made it back when you were just a child."

"Does that create a problem?"

"Not really. Obviously, you've reached the age

of majority, so you'll inherit directly. The house, the business, Angie's savings..."

Drew looked down at the hardwood floor at his feet. The finish was faded, like everything else in this almost-century-old house. He loved this place, but what was he going to do with it?

Same with the newspaper. Angie had put it out every week that he could remember. Before that, her father had done the same. What was to become of it now? As far as he knew, no one was interested in buying it.

A hand reached for his. Mallory's. She squeezed tightly. "You don't have to worry about everything right now, Drew. Things will sort themselves out."

He understood what she meant. There were more immediate concerns. "What about...what about funeral arrangements? Does the will say anything about that? About what Angie wanted?"

"No. But Angie wasn't one for pomp and circumstance."

"Cremation?" He had to choke out the word.

"Probably. And a memorial service. There'll be a lot of people who want to pay their respects."

"We'll hold a wake." Drew didn't know he'd made his mind up until the words were out.

The three of them looked around the table at one another.

"You'll have to pass around Angie's homemade brandy," Mallory said.

Drew grinned. "There'll be music. And I'm going to run a commemorative issue of the *Gazette*." Again, the words were out before he realized he'd thought them. But everything was sounding right. Buddy looked as if he thought so, too.

"You won't have to worry about food. Believe me, once people hear what you're doing, the food will come to you."

BUDDY WAS RIGHT, as Mallory had known he would be. Monday morning she opened the door to find Drew standing there with two baking tins in his hands.

"Can I put these in your fridge? Mine is already jammed with salads and casseroles."

"Sure." She stood back to let him pass, wiping her damp hands on the front of her jeans. She'd just washed her face and was battling another wave of nausea, but seeing Drew on her doorstep made her smile.

As usual.

Angie had always said her son was too handsome for his own good, and probably she was right, but Mallory had never thought of him as exceptionally attractive. What she did notice was his smile, and the way he energized any room the moment he walked in. Then there were his eyes. Just looking at them, you knew he had to be a journalist. They saw so much.

"Want some coffee?" she offered. The smell would make her stomach crazy, but the discomfort would be worth it to have his company for a few minutes. She'd worried about him last night, his first night alone in Angie's house. She wished he would have agreed to stay another couple of nights with her.

"No, thanks. I made some at Angie's." He shut the fridge, then turned and leaned against it. Shoving his hands in the pockets of his jeans, he tilted his head and smiled at her. "Sleep okay last night? You looked done for when I left at eight."

She shrugged. Exhaustion had been the first symptom of her pregnancy. At the end of each day it was all she could do to keep her eyes open while she ate her evening meal. Last night with Drew, she'd struggled to stay alert while they shared their pizza. A movie had been out of the question.

"How did *you* sleep?" she asked.

He glanced down. "Okay, I guess."

Impulsively, she walked over and put her hand on his shoulder. "It must be so hard."

She was thinking of Angie, of course, and of his loss, but the moment she touched him she felt oddly confused. Their eyes locked and his hand reached up to her waist. If he hadn't done that, she would have stepped back, but she was effectively pinned, and she felt the heat from his body and the press of his shoulder and thigh against her skin.

This is Drew, she tried to tell herself, but she couldn't keep the air in her lungs, and her head felt as though it were floating.

He hadn't shaved. There was something intimate and sensual about the dark stubble on his face. And about his lips. How many times had those lips laughed at her and teased her? Now all she could remember was what it had felt like to kiss him.

"Drew." She said his name because she wanted to ground them, both in their friendship and their past. But instead the word came out sounding like a request for something she'd wanted for a very long time.

She closed her eyes and dropped her forehead lightly against his chest. "It must be so hard," she said again, and this time when she moved her leg backward, he dropped his hand and let her go.

"I wish I'd been able to tell her goodbye. I wish I'd been there to hold her hand at the hospital."

Drew looked at his own hand, as though it could somehow link him to his mother. "Damn it, I wish I'd done a hundred things differently. Why did Angie have to die alone?"

Mallory shook her head. She had no answers. At one time she would have simply given Drew a hug. But what had happened by the fridge frightened her. She didn't feel ready to touch him again.

"Do you think she was scared, Mal? Do you think she asked for me before she lost consciousness?"

"I bet you were the last thought in her mind, Drew. And I think that must have been very comforting to her."

Mallory felt tears on her face as she imagined those last conscious moments of Angie's life. She knew it was selfish, but she couldn't help thinking how much she herself would miss Angie. Angie had given her the warmth and unquestioning acceptance she had never found at home with her aunt Norma.

Maybe she had had it once with her real parents, but her memories of them were was so faded now. She could only recollect snatches of their time together: a song her mother had sung to her in the bath, her father carrying her on his shoulders, the color of their kitchen walls. Bright yellow.

"When I called the hospital, they said she fell unconscious shortly after she was admitted. She didn't *know* she was alone, Drew." Mallory reached for the box of tissues she kept on the counter and passed one to Drew. He wasn't crying, but his eyes looked red. She blew her nose, then splashed water on her face from the kitchen faucet.

When she turned off the tap, Drew passed her the towel she kept tucked in the fridge handle.

"Have I ever told you you're my best friend in the whole wide world?" he said.

She smiled. They'd told each other that when they were kids. They'd had a secret handshake to go with the words, and now she held out her hands to him.

First they clasped their right hands, then their left, forming an *x* between them. Best friends. But how was he going to feel when he found out she was pregnant? And when was there ever going to be a right time to tell him?

MALLORY SPENT THE DAY making pumpkin pies, the sight and smell of the pureed pumpkin sending her to the bathroom, gagging, more than once. When they had cooled she loaded them in a cardboard box and carried them out to her car. Drew was sitting on his back deck, reading a newspaper.

"I'm off to Claire's. Want a ride?" She leaned over the raspberry hedge, balancing the box in her hands.

"No, thanks. I'll come up later." He folded the paper over and she saw a headline: Tensions Mount In Middle East.

"Was that the story you were supposed to cover?"

"Yeah. It made the front page."

Mallory felt the keen bite of his disappointment, saw it on his face. While Drew had reported on many key political events, none of his articles had been national front-page news. She knew that getting his byline on the front page was one of his goals. And now he'd missed a perfect opportunity.

He glanced at the box she held. "What have you got there? Smells good."

"You'll have to wait and see." She moved on to her car, setting the box on the floor of the back seat, then waved at him before backing out of the garage.

As she drove the familiar route, she again thought of the disappointment etched on Drew's face that second before he'd pulled himself together. Of course he'd have other chances....

She wondered how long he was planning to stay in Port Carling. They hadn't talked about that yet.

Claire was alone in the kitchen of the Ridgeway cottage when Mallory arrived. Mallory set the box of pies on the counter that divided the cozy kitchen from the large dining cum living room. The cottage faced west, toward the lake, and windows lined that wall, providing a spectacular view. A long pine table, capable of seating at least twenty, filled the north section of the room, while several comfy couches and chairs nested around the stone fireplace on the south wall.

"Is that your famous black-bean-and-corn salad you're making?" Mallory asked.

"None other." Claire continued to chop fine green cilantro leaves. She was wearing a jean shirt with pumpkins embroidered on the collar, and dark-blue leggings with her desert boots. Her sleek blond hair was pulled back in a ponytail, highlighting the delicate lines of her fine features.

Mallory slid onto the stool opposite her. "Claire,

you can't announce my pregnancy at the dinner tonight.''

Claire stopped chopping and looked at Mallory. "Why not? It's the perfect time, with everyone together.''

"I'm just not ready. Please, Claire."

"It's Angie, isn't it?"

"Yes." Of course that was part of it. Mallory couldn't tell Drew when his grief over his mother's death was still so raw. And she couldn't tell anyone else until she'd told him.

"I wonder what's going to happen to the *Gazette?*'' Claire resumed chopping the cilantro, her knife falling against the wooden cutting board with dull regularity. "Has Drew mentioned his plans?"

Mallory plucked a piece of chopped green pepper from the bowl. "It's too soon. I think he's feeling completely overwhelmed.''

"Port Carling won't be the same place without the *Gazette*—those editorials, the community page, especially Angie's cottage cooking column." Claire scraped the cilantro into her salad. "Angie couldn't cook to save her life. How she came up with those recipes I'll never know.''

"Of course you know, Claire. You gave her half of them.''

Claire stared at her blankly, as if she'd forgotten she'd ever done such a thing.

"Just think how hard this must be for Drew. He

feels so bad about not coming home on Thursday as planned. And the cancer was just as much of a shock for him as it was for us. I wonder why Angie never told him.''

Claire glanced up from the open oven. ''Do you really?''

''Of course.'' Mallory frowned. ''What do you mean by that?''

''Oh, nothing. Could you help me with this roaster, please? This bird is enormous.''

Mallory grabbed an oven mitt and they carried the roaster to the counter. ''Wow, this is heavy. How big is it?''

''Twenty pounds,'' Claire assured her. ''Although right now it feels more like fifty.''

''It looks fantastic.'' The skin was golden-brown and shimmered with the baked-on basting sauce Claire always used.

''You should taste the dressing. Here, have a bite.''

Mallory closed her eyes and opened her mouth. The flavors of poultry seasoning blended with the tang of cranberries and a touch of brandy. Her teeth bit through soft bread crumbs, then encountered the crunch of hazelnuts and celery. ''Claire, you really have outdone yourself this time. Is there a recipe?''

''Not yet. I haven't had time to write it out.'' Claire passed Mallory a spoon and a pretty pottery bowl. "Here, scoop this out of the cavity, will you? I want to see if my cranberry-jelly mold set."

"Promise me you'll be able to replicate this," Mallory said, sneaking another bite. "For next year when I won't be throwing up everything I eat."

"Oh, Mallory. Have you been sick a lot?" Claire, who'd sailed through each of her three pregnancies with ease, had the good grace to appear sheepish.

"Only morning, noon and night."

"It should end soon, now that you're past your first trimester."

"I hope so."

The front door opened, and a gust of fall air blew in some stray leaves. Soon, Kirk and the three girls were tramping into the house.

"We found lots of pinecones and leaves, Mommy," Daisy, the six-year-old, said.

"Great. You guys can make the centerpiece for the table. Just arrange all your treasures around the pumpkin Daddy carved this morning."

The cottage was already a treasure trove of the girls' crafts. Taped to the windows were paper turkeys—tail feathers really cutouts of small hands— and pressed fall leaves. The fridge was covered with drawings, and animals made out of pinecones lined the stone mantel of the fireplace.

"The kids treat me like a criminal if I try to throw away a toilet-paper roll," Claire had once complained to Mallory. "Do you know anyone else who has twenty old egg cartons in her back closet?"

Mallory had wondered if a day would come when she'd be asked to save such treasures. Now, amazingly, it seemed it would.

"It's turned brisk out there," Kirk said, rubbing his hands together. "Do you need help in the kitchen?"

It struck Mallory that Claire looked at him coolly before replying.

"Everything's under control. Why don't you get the glue gun and help the girls. People should be arriving any minute now."

Sure enough, the center-piece had only just been created when a knock sounded at the door. It was Grady and Bess, with their twin boys, Taylor and Warren. The boys had turned fifteen this summer, and Mallory, who saw them every couple of weeks or so, still couldn't believe how tall they'd grown.

"Here's a salad." Bess dumped a white plastic bowl of tossed greens on Claire's counter.

"Thanks, Bess." Claire raised her eyebrows as she passed Mallory on the way to the fridge, and Mallory pushed down a smile.

Bess and Claire had never seemed to get past polite tolerance of each other's presence. Mallory had no idea why the two women were so naturally antagonistic, although she was willing to acknowledge that Bess could be cool and bristly at times. And

Claire was a snob about cooking, although she would never admit it. Sometimes, Mallory suspected that Bess's casually prepared and presented offerings were calculated to raise Claire's ire.

"Drew was right behind me, in his mom's car," Grady said.

On cue, Drew's step sounded on the flagstone stairs. He came in wearing jeans and a white shirt, open at the neck, and carrying a couple of bottles of wine.

"Hey, Drew." Kirk clasped him on the shoulder. "I'm really sorry. I was so shocked to hear about your mother."

"You weren't the only one."

Drew's mouth had a bitter twist, and Mallory could see the signs of lack of sleep in the dark skin under his eyes and the lines furrowing the corners of his mouth.

Grady walked up to offer a beer. He'd already dropped by Drew's to express his condolences. Now it was obvious he thought it best to change the subject. "Tell us, Kirk, how are the markets doing?"

So like men to avoid the sticky emotional issues, Mallory thought, watching them stand around the fireplace and listen to Kirk explain how their portfolios were doing. She sighed and returned to the kitchen, where Claire was making gravy. The kids had all run outside to the tire swings, even the twins,

whom she might have expected to consider themselves too old for such play.

Everyone was involved in something except Bess.
She'd accepted a glass of wine from Kirk and was
sitting in an armchair across the room, staring into
the fireplace as Kirk fussed with the kindling, still
talking investments over his shoulder to the two
other guys.

Dinner was a feast, as only Claire's cooking de-
fined the word. Besides the turkey and dressing,
Claire's two salads and Bess's limp greens, there
were garlic mashed potatoes, sweet potatoes gar-
nished with brown-sugar glaze and pecans, julienned
turnips and carrots and a jar of Angie's applesauce.

No one had room for pumpkin pie afterward, but
they all took a slice.

The festive mood cratered slightly when Taylor
interrupted his father's description of a beautiful old
boat he was working on. "Can we go home soon?"

Grady's lips compressed. "No. Not for a while.
Why don't you boys go outside and find something
to do."

"If you can keep those kids from following us,"
Warren said.

Claire's face reddened, and Mallory cringed. She
caught Drew's eye from across the table and saw
that he was puzzled by the rude behavior. So was
she. Taylor and Warren were usually so good-
natured with the younger kids.

Once the children had left the table, the adults lingered over coffee. By this time conversation had shifted to Drew, and everyone wanted to catch up on his most recent travels and experiences. When it came time to do the dishes, Bess got up from the table.

"I think I should take the boys home now."

As Grady stood to leave, she waved him back into his seat.

"You stay and catch up with your friends. Drew, could Grady catch a ride home with you?"

"Sure. No problem." Drew placed an arm across Grady's shoulders. "The boys are sure growing up."

"Yeah. Too fast." Grady settled back into his chair. Mallory noticed him watching Bess—he didn't appear happy that she was leaving. "Seemed to happen all at once. Where did all the years go?"

"I've been wondering the same thing."

Mallory threw a dishcloth at Grady, a clean tea towel at Drew. "How come men always want to philosophize when it's time to do the dishes?"

"I'd have thought the answer to that was obvious," Grady grumbled, but he still took his place by the sink.

Claire gathered her girls, put on their coats and organized their weekend bags. Kirk was taking them back to Toronto so he could go to work and they could go to school. His mother was going to help out for the extra three days that Claire would be away.

"I'll be home Thursday night," Claire said. She kissed Jenna on the cheek, then buttoned her coat. "Remember to brush your teeth before you go to bed."

Mallory stopped scraping and stacking dishes long enough to kiss the girls goodbye, too.

"I'll call you when we get in," Kirk said on his way out the door.

"Good."

Mallory noticed that Claire hadn't met his eyes as she'd answered him. And while she'd kissed each one of the girls, she hadn't gone near Kirk. Something was going on here. And Mallory didn't like the look of it.

CHAPTER FOUR

BUDDY CONROY SAT in the fifth pew from the front, his wife by his side, and wished he could have convinced Angie to tell her son that she was sick before it had been too late. He'd felt terrible helping Drew go through the business of death, when it was obvious the boy was still in shock at the news.

Buddy could imagine what he felt. Sorrow at having missed the opportunity for final farewells, as well as guilt for not being there at the end. Angie shouldn't have done this to Drew, or to her friends, either.

But as far as Buddy knew, he was the only person she'd told. "Why put my burden on other people's shoulders?" she'd asked him when he'd questioned her about the secrecy. "I feel bad enough telling you...."

He was glad she had. Carrying the burden all on her own would have been inhuman. Reluctantly, he'd respected her request not to tell anyone else— not even his wife. Now he glanced at Patricia, wearing her dark-blue funeral suit, even though he'd cautioned her that Drew wanted a celebration for Angie, not a mourning.

Thirty-five years he and Patricia had been married. They'd raised two children and built a life together. In all those years he'd never been unfaithful, never even kept a secret from her. Except this one. Angie's cancer.

Organ music swelled from the front of the church, drowning out the sound of feet shuffling, the private whispers and occasional cough. The mournful melody connected with the sadness in the air, shaping it into an almost palpable thing.

Buddy glanced around the church. The ceremony would be private, preceding the larger wake that was to follow in the Driscoll family home. Drew was sitting near the front, his friends by his side. He was somber, and hadn't quite lost the look of stunned surprise that had been so evident when Buddy had met him to go over the details of the will.

Behind Drew were a couple of Angie's friends from Toronto, and in the pews behind them sat the employees from the *Gazette* and their families.

The organ music stopped, and the minister stood up to speak. He placed both hands on the pulpit and leaned forward to tell the small congregation, ''There is a season for all things.''

Buddy believed in that. But Angie's death was a travesty. He couldn't see her passing as part of the natural order of things. She was too young—not yet sixty—with the spirit and energy of someone at least twenty years younger. She'd given so much to the community—through the *Gazette* and her involvement in almost every committee you could think of, and had still had so much to contribute. She'd done a wonderful job raising Drew, and she'd been a good friend to many people.

Including him.

At the front of the room, the minister was now quoting from Proverbs: "'A good name is to be chosen rather than great riches, Loving favor rather than silver and gold.'"

Patricia squeezed Buddy's hand, and he returned the pressure. *A good name.* Yes, Angie had had that. As for silver and gold, well, monetary possessions had always been pretty low priorities. Not that she hadn't lived a comfortable life.

Buddy lowered his head, unable to focus on the words of acceptance, as the minister began to pray. Angie Driscoll, six years his junior, was dead. In her life she'd made a big difference to the people of Port Carling, working to protect the quality of life they all enjoyed. But what about her personal hopes and desires?

Buddy knew her greatest longings had been for her son. She'd worried about his restless nature, the edge of dissatisfaction that occasionally peeked out from behind his charming facade.

She'd taken great pride in Drew's professional

success, yet would have loved nothing more than to see him married to a loving wife, starting a family of his own. Angie was like every other mother in her wishes for her child.

But Drew had been living the life of a roving journalist for more than a decade now. Maybe he wouldn't ever settle down.

And if he did, it would be too late for Angie to enjoy it. Life was so damn unfair. Angie had been cheated. And what about the rest of them? Buddy couldn't imagine what life was going to be like without her.

THEY'D THOUGHT OF EVERYTHING for his mother's wake, Drew figured. There was music from a local Celtic folk trio, tons of food and of course Angie's homemade brandy. Not to mention a commemorative issue of the *Hub of the Lakes Gazette*.

He'd slaved day and night to get the issue ready for Wednesday. Poring over thirty-odd years' worth of articles and editorials, he'd felt as though he was reliving his own life, as well as his mother's. He'd picked out his favorites, done some writing of his own, then patched it all together.

"I just finished reading your commemorative issue, Drew. It's absolutely wonderful." Mallory came up from behind him as he was putting some potted flowers on the living-room coffee table.

"I hope she would have liked it." Drew turned

from the flowers, which were a tribute to Angie from the *Gazette* staff, and looked at the paper in Mallory's hands. "It's been a long time since I was responsible for things like layout, headlines and graphic design."

"Well, you haven't lost the touch."

"Thanks, Mal." Her praise meant a lot. "And thanks for everything you've done these past few days. I don't know how I would have made it through them without you."

"I was glad to help."

He studied her. Same warm smile, same level gaze. Was he imagining the reserve in her voice? If so, it wasn't the first time these past few days.

He reached for one of her hands and gave it a squeeze. It felt cold and stiff, and a second later, Mallory pulled it out of his grasp.

Odd. He remembered their conversation in the car on the way in from the airport. They still hadn't talked about whatever it was bothering her. After the funeral, she'd said. Well, this was after the funeral, wasn't it?

"Tell me what the problem is, Mal."

She averted her gaze, bent to admire the flowers he'd just put down. "Besides Angie, you mean?"

Was that what he was sensing in her? Grief over Angie? He didn't think so; she was being evasive.

"You still don't feel like talking, do you?"

"Not here. Not now."

Drew's gut churned. For an instant he felt angry. Mallory was a constant he'd thought he could depend on. The same way he depended on Grady and Claire, only more so. He and Mallory had always been especially close. After all, they'd grown up together.

He wanted her to stay the same.

"Isn't the music great? Where did you find the band?"

Drew paused a second. Getting mad at Mallory wouldn't solve anything. Whatever it was that was bothering her, they'd work out. Eventually.

"Grady heard them in one of the local bars. He got their phone number for me. They say this is their first funeral—"

"You mean wake."

"Right." That made him smile. "Wake. Do you think we'll have enough food?"

That made *her* smile, since both of their refrigerators had ended up stuffed with contributions from friends and neighbors.

"You have enough food to feed all of Port Carling for a week. Claire is absolutely in her element arranging all those casseroles and squares on the dining-room table. I think she brought a casserole of her own, even though I told her we wouldn't need it."

"As if Claire would pass up the opportunity to cook."

"That's true. Especially with all that leftover turkey. By the way, did you talk to Angie's friends from Toronto before they left? It was nice of them to drive all this way."

"It was, wasn't it? And yes, we had the opportunity to chat. I had a few questions—"

"About that day?" Mallory asked tactfully. Referring, of course, to the day Angie had died.

He nodded. "Angie met her friends at an Italian restaurant in Yorkville. When she arrived, she was obviously in terrible pain. She told her friends that her headache started shortly after she'd left Port Carling."

"Such a long trip." Mallory shook her head. "If only she'd asked...I would have been happy to drive her."

"Her friends offered her pain tablets, but Angie said she'd taken some pretty strong drugs already, and that she was certain she'd feel better soon."

"But she didn't."

"No. She ended up deciding to go back to her hotel room without eating. Of course her friends now feel terrible, that they didn't go with her. But they couldn't have known..."

How could they, when Angie hadn't told anyone how sick she was? Except maybe Buddy. Drew had his suspicions there.

"Did Angie make it to the hotel?"

"Just. She collapsed in the lobby. The manager

sent for an ambulance, and we know what happened after that...."

Everyone he'd spoken to today felt some measure of regret that they hadn't been able to help Angie. But for him, the burden was greater. He was her son and he had let her down.

"Drew." Mallory's hand was on his arm. "Do you remember when you took your mom for a ride on a hot-air balloon for her fiftieth birthday?"

"Sure." His mother had put a picture on the cover of the *Gazette* that week, she'd been so proud.

"She told me that you always knew how to make her happy." Mallory squeezed his arms. "So stop thinking you weren't a good son, okay? Because you were."

"God, Mal." He put his arm over her shoulders and had to blink several times. "You're going to make me cry, you know that?"

"It's allowed."

"You know what I've been wondering?"

"What?"

"If maybe Angie didn't tell me she was sick because she didn't want me asking questions she didn't want to answer."

"Oh? Like what?"

"Questions like how I happened to be born and why she never married. I don't know that much about my mother's life before she started working at the *Gazette*," he admitted. "I know she went to college for a couple of years. I know there was some grand passion before she left Port Carling.''

''I've never heard about that.''

''Neither had Angie's old school friends. When I asked, they said Angie never talked about him. I guess the affair was truly over by the time she went to Toronto.''

''What else did you ask Angie's friends about?''

''My father,'' he said bluntly. ''I knew Angie hadn't dated him for long, but I was hoping they might have met him once.''

''And had they?''

He shook his head. ''Never. Do you know what else they told me?''

Mallory's pale eyebrows rose.

''Angie's dream was to be a foreign correspondent when she graduated. She wanted travel, excitement and unpredictability.''

''Doesn't that sound familiar.''

Exactly what he'd wanted. And still did. Only, he'd never known his mother had had the same dreams.

''But then she got pregnant.'' God, it was too ironic that because of *him* she'd given up on her plans. And how did he repay her? By leaving Port Carling only days after high-school graduation.

''She told me she moved back because of your grandfather's health,'' Mallory interjected. ''He had a stroke about a month before her graduation.''

So maybe a combination of events had led Angie back to this town. "She turned down an offer from the *Toronto Star* to come home."

"Really?"

"According to her friends. That must have been hard." Drew clenched the back of his grandpa's old leather chair. His mother had given up so much for her family. Would she have expected the same from him in similar circumstances? That he would pick up the reins when she passed on? Return to Port Carling and keep the family paper going?

Oh, Angie! Why didn't you talk to me about any of this?

AN HOUR LATER, DREW STARTED handing out glasses and offering people shots from his mother's brandy bottle. It was time to give a toast. His mother had always been very big on toasts.

"Come on, Buddy," he said, patting the lawyer on the back. "This one's for Angie. The best mother a guy could ever ask for."

"For your mother," Buddy echoed. "The most damn amazing woman this town has ever seen."

Drew found his friends standing around the dining-room table, where Claire was cutting a pan of brownies into squares.

"Here you are. I should have known you'd be hovering around the food. Be careful, now. Mal and I are planning to eat for weeks on the leftovers." As he spoke, he passed out more glasses, then began to fill them. He was surprised when Mallory refused.

"No, thanks, Drew. My, um, my stomach is a little unsettled. I don't think I should—"

"Nonsense. Brandy is just the thing for an unsettled stomach, isn't it, Claire?"

"Well, sometimes." Claire straightened and set down her knife. "But in this case Mallory would probably really like some peppermint tea. Wouldn't you, Mallory?"

"Peppermint tea? When you can drink Angie's raspberry brandy? I don't think so." Drew held the bottle to Mallory's glass once more. This time she let him fill it.

Then he turned to Grady, who'd been talking to Patricia Conroy by a bowl of heated meatballs at the other end of the table.

"Let's drink to Angie's accomplishments," Grady suggested, raising the glass that Drew had just filled.

Obligingly, Drew brought his own glass to his lips. The brandy felt warm and rich coursing down his throat. Just then Taylor and Warren came into the room and made for their father.

"Can we go home, Dad?" asked Warren. "We're bored."

Grady's gaze flew to Drew, then back to his sons. "Come on, guys. Where're your manners?"

Warren didn't look apologetic. "You said we'd only have to stay an hour or two."

Grady's chest expanded as he took a deep breath, and Drew felt sorry for his friend. Teenagers. At least he didn't have to deal with problems like that.

"What do you say I get out my laptop computer for you guys?" he proposed. "I've got some games that might be kind of fun."

"Maybe another time." This was Taylor. "We made plans with some of our friends."

Drew shrugged. Friends. Well, they were at that age, weren't they? He'd noticed the change this summer when he was down for his holiday. Several times the twins had turned down invitations from their father to join the two of them on their fishing or waterskiing excursions.

Yet hadn't he and Grady been the same when they were fifteen? Except maybe not quite that rude.

"Don't worry about it," he said to Grady now. "Let them go visit their friends."

As the twins were filing out, he noticed Mallory slip into the kitchen. She had her brandy glass with her, and it was still full. He followed, then stood silently behind her as she poured the liquid into the sink and rinsed her glass.

She started when she turned and saw him.

"Drew! What are you doing here?"

"You really didn't want that brandy, did you, Mal?"

She closed her eyes and sucked in a deep breath. ''Drew. There's something we need to talk about. But I'm not sure if now—''

He stepped forward and took hold of her wrist. He hadn't meant to be rough, but she pulled back from him, eyes open wide.

''That hurt.''

''What's going on, Mallory? You said we needed to talk—well, let's do it. Ever since I came home, you've been acting strange. All tense and uptight. And you're on this weird health kick where you can't eat and you won't drink coffee or alcohol—''

Words ran out on him as the significance of what he'd just said struck him. She'd been sick that morning when he'd spent the night in her spare room.... Oh, God, was it possible?

''You're pregnant, aren't you.''

CHAPTER FIVE

MALLORY COULD TELL DREW was praying he was wrong, but she confirmed his guess with a nod.

"Yes. I'm pregnant."

"Oh, my God." He looked at her waist, cinched in with a gold belt, and she knew he was thinking that it was as slender as always. Her hands rose instinctively to her flat belly.

"I'm not showing yet. I'm only three months along."

"Three months." Drew's gaze returned to her face. She could see him counting backward in his mind, his eyes widening when he stopped at July. "So that weekend—"

"Yes. That weekend."

He stepped backward. "But I used protection. I'm sure I remember."

So did she. Or thought she did. The first time, definitely. The second time, she wasn't as sure. Truth was, her memory of that day was textured with so many feelings and discoveries that focusing in on any one detail was difficult. Possibly, they'd both been a little careless because of the friendship and the trust between them. Or maybe fate had been at work.

Drew walked to the sink and ran a glass of water, which he downed in one swallow. Then he hung his head, pausing a long moment before brushing back his hair and facing her again.

"Pregnant. You're sure about this? There isn't any mistake?"

"Of course I'm sure." Mallory ran her thumb over the smooth face of her watch, then twisted the metal band back and forth. Not to resent the question took effort. She had to remind herself that he was in shock. This was his mother's wake, for heaven's sake; she shouldn't have let him bully her into telling him now.

But it was too late to do anything about that. Besides, it was just as well he knew. This was reality, and it needed facing.

"Pregnant," he repeated, as if trying to get used to the idea.

She watched as he tilted his head back, lifting his gaze to the ceiling. Her eyes followed, and absurdly, she noticed a small crack that needed to be patched. This house wasn't in bad shape, considering its age, but Angie had never worried about day-to-day maintenance. If Drew was going to sell, there was some work that needed to be done.

Oh, Lord. The reality of the situation hit her then. He was going to sell this house and close the paper.

Without Angie, he'd have little reason to visit Port Carling. Everything would change, had already begun to change.

Now his attention was back on her. "I should have guessed. The signs were there, starting with the drive home from the airport when you couldn't eat that burger and shake. I've been such a blind fool."

"Hey, your mind was on other things."

His chest expanded as he took a deep breath. "Three months. Jeez, Mallory. Why didn't you tell me sooner?"

"I didn't know for sure until about six weeks ago when I took one of those home pregnancy tests. I had the results confirmed with a blood test a few weeks later."

"Six weeks. Seems you could have picked up the phone in that amount of time."

He was angry and she couldn't blame him. Not really.

"I didn't want to tell you over the phone. I put it off long enough that it seemed easier to wait until Thanksgiving, when you'd be here and I could tell you in person."

He laughed, and the sound was bitter. "But then, of course, I canceled my plans to come home for the holiday."

"I realized I'd have to phone you then. But before I got a chance, Angie died...."

Her gaze dropped to his white shirt. He'd worn a

tie to the service but had taken it off right after. Now, where he'd loosened a couple of buttons, she could see a patch of browned skin, lightly covered by dark curly hair.

"And here I am. God, Mallory. How many people know about this already?"

"I've told Claire—but no one else. I've been waiting to tell you first..."

"So why didn't you say something on the drive back from the airport?"

Mallory sank down on a nearby chair. She could understand his anger, but this was beginning to feel like an inquisition. "I thought you had enough on your plate dealing with Angie's death."

"Still, I wish you'd have said something."

"Maybe I should have, but I was scared."

"Scared?" He sat opposite her, resting his elbows on the table and cupping his head in his hands. "Why would you be scared?"

"I don't know. I guess I was worried you might want me to terminate the pregnancy." Just saying the word *terminate* gave her the shivers.

"Which you don't want to do?"

"No," she said quickly. "Of course not."

"And you thought I might have tried to force you?"

"No." Mallory picked at a flake of pastry on the table, shredding it into bits.

"I sure as hell hope not." He sat for a few

minutes, drumming his fingers on the table. When he looked up again, his forehead was creased. ''What are we going to do, Mal?''

He looked so overwhelmed. And why not? He was at his mother's wake and he'd just found out he was about to become a father. ''Please don't worry. It's going to be okay.''

She could see Drew swallow, his Adam's apple traveling down his throat and then up again.

''You want to keep the baby?''

''Yes.'' She leaned forward and began to speak quickly. ''I can afford it, Drew. My job at the store is flexible. I can take the baby with me some of the time. And I'll hire extra help when I need it.''

Drew rubbed a hand along the side of his face, then leaned back in his chair. ''You sound like you have this all figured out.''

''I'm not asking you for anything, Drew. Not money, or support, or even for you to be involved. Unless you want to be. You could be like a favorite uncle or a family friend. We wouldn't have to tell anyone that you're the father.''

''But I am the father?'' His look was direct now. ''There's no doubt?''

''Of course you're the father. What kind of question is that?'' Mallory glared at him, heat pulsing in her cheeks.

''I'm sorry. I didn't mean to offend you. It's just,

well, I know you were going out with this other guy for a while..."

"That was six months ago. And just because I was going out with Randall doesn't mean—" Mallory paused, then shook her head. Drew with all his women, how would he understand? Still, that he would ask something like that...

"Don't you think I would have said something if there was any doubt you were the father?" Mallory stood, pushing her chair aside, and moved to the sink. In the dark of night, the kitchen window acted as a mirror, and she saw him follow her, then felt his arms on her shoulders. She turned her gaze down to the soapy water in the sink, wishing she'd never even told him about the baby. He was spoiling everything with all these questions.

"I'm sorry," he said again, using his hands to pivot her toward him. He stroked the side of her cheek. "Of course I believe you. There's no question of that. I just had to ask."

Mallory tried to understand. But still she felt disappointed, sad. And angry at herself for feeling that way. She'd never expected Drew to leap for joy when he heard the news. Understandably, he'd be shocked, even angry that it had taken her so long to tell him. All things considered, he was taking this rather calmly.

She'd have to be a fool to have hoped for anything more.

"And you're sure about keeping the baby?"

"Yes. I'm sure."

"Okay, then. That's what we'll do." He took her hand in his and squeezed it. "How are you feeling? I mean, obviously you've been tired and sick. Is all that normal?"

"Pretty much. At least according to my doctor and Claire."

"Two authorities—no doubt about that." He released her hand and eyed her for a long moment.

She wondered what he was thinking, but he gave no sign. After a few moments he sighed and moved away from her.

"There's a houseful of people for me to see to right now. But I need to talk to you again. Soon."

"Okay."

"Coming?" He arched an eyebrow.

She shook her head. "In a minute."

Once he was gone, she collapsed into a chair. Thank goodness he finally knew and she no longer had to keep this secret between them.

But, oh, that look on his face when he'd realized it was true, that she was going to have his baby. As if he'd been crushed. To him, her pregnancy was just another problem to add to his load.

Mallory stroked her tummy, as though to protect her child from the knowledge that one of the people who'd created her wasn't exactly thrilled about it.

She ought to be fair about this. What man in

Drew's situation would be thrilled at the news? Surely she hadn't expected him to break out in a big silly grin. To throw his arms around her and exclaim, "We're going to have a baby!"

After all, they weren't lovers—even though they had made love that one weekend. She'd come home from that experience in shock. She was nothing like the glamorous women Drew dated; she'd never thought he would be able to feel…that way…about her.

Yet he had. For one weekend they'd crossed the boundary from friends to lovers. And that had scared her, because Drew's lovers came and then went.

Her first worry had been for their friendship— could it survive? She'd known that on some level things would never be the same between them, even though she'd promised him that nothing would change.

But that was before she'd known she was going to have his baby.

CHAPTER SIX

THE NEXT MORNING DREW opened the back door to stack cartons of empty bottles on the deck. If the quantity of alcohol consumed was any indication, the party had been a hell of a one.

Drew's head ached. Too much of Angie's brandy the night before. And too little sleep.

"You look a bit rough." Mallory's voice traveled through the screen of raspberry canes. He straightened, and saw her sitting on her deck, a carafe and two mugs on the table beside her. "Come over and have some coffee. Then I'll help you clean up."

"Did you say coffee?" He eased past the hedge, with Doug on his heels. Mallory was stretched out on an old wooden lounge chair she'd had for years. Sometime recently she'd painted it turquoise.

The morning sun made her brown hair glow like a halo. He pushed a hand down on the top of her head, a move that normally annoyed her. Sure enough, she grimaced. "Sit and try not to make a nuisance of yourself for a change."

She sounded so cross he had to smile. "Sounds like you haven't had *your* dose of caffeine yet."

She shook her head. "I'm not drinking coffee. This is herbal tea."

Herbal tea. Of course. He was an idiot. Automatically, his eyes fell to the midsection of her denim overalls. He'd seen her wear them before, but today his first thought was that they were perfect for concealing the initial stages of pregnancy. Not that there was any need for concealment. As Mallory had pointed out, she wasn't showing yet. But soon she would be.

Even after a night to adjust, he found it hard to believe a baby was growing inside Mallory. More specifically, a fetus, a three-month-old fetus. Drew's forehead creased as he felt the reality of the situation.

Don't think about it. He stepped closer to Mallory and peered into the mug she held in her hand. The liquid it held was a suspicious color. "No wonder you're in such a foul mood."

"There's coffee in the carafe. Real coffee."

Sure enough, the strong rich smell of ground Colombian beans wafted into the air as he twisted open the top of the carafe, then poured the dark brew into his mug.

"You're a lifesaver." He sank onto the chair next to hers—this one a bright yellow—and propped his feet against a tub of red, pink and white geraniums.

Doug came to rest his head on the arm of the chair, and Drew scratched behind the dog's ears.

There was something so pathetic about the way the old retriever had started following him around. Looking at him, seeing the questions that seemed to glow from those dark-brown eyes, hurt Drew.

Where was Angie? Would she come home soon?

Drew knew just how he felt. The house was so empty and quiet without his mother.

"What time did everyone leave?"

Mallory had stuck it out until midnight, which was when the dancing had started. Irish jigs. They'd pushed back the sofa and rolled up the living-room rug.

"Grady stayed until six. He was the last to go."

"Trust Grady," Mallory said with a laugh. "Did you get any sleep?"

"A little," he lied. After Grady had left, Drew had sat in his grandfather's old chair, thinking. It was all so bloody unfair, so bloody unexpected. One week ago he'd been a man in the prime of his career, his future a golden path before him. Now his world had fallen apart and he didn't know what to worry about first—the paper, the house, Doug or the baby. God, he was a mess.

"Drew, trust me. It's going to be okay."

"Oh, Mal." She always knew, didn't she? "I feel so bloody selfish. Worrying about myself, when you've got so much to deal with."

"I'm happy about this baby, Drew. Really I am."

And the truth was, she did look happy. Well, if not happy, then at least content.

"Aren't you scared?"

"A little, I guess. But in an excited kind of way."

He tried, but he couldn't quite believe it. "I guess I should get back to cleaning. I don't want you helping, though. You should stay out here with your feet up. You know, rest or something."

She just smiled as she rose from her chair. "Drew, I'm fine."

"You won't be once you see the mess inside." He led the way to his back door, but at the threshold he paused, suddenly paralyzed by lethargy. He'd worked so hard these past few days, organizing the memorial service and the wake, printing the commemorative issue of the *Gazette*. The stress had sucked the energy out of him.

Now the sight of leftover food on the counter, crumbs on the floor and dirty casserole dishes in the sink was almost too much to bear.

"You know, we don't have to do this now."

Mallory was right behind him, and he had an overpowering, inexplicable urge to pull her into his arms and squeeze her against him. He wanted to feel the rough texture of her hair against his cheek, the creamy softness of her cheek on his chest.

Turning, he saw her looking at him, her eyes wide with sympathy and caring. All he had to do was hold out his arms and he knew she'd fall into them. But was it only comfort he was seeking? He was quite certain that was all she was offering.

"What the hell are we going to do?" he asked, not even sure who he was talking to—himself or Mallory.

"Is it the baby?"

He had to avert his gaze, didn't know what to say.

"I don't have to keep this baby, Drew, but I want to. As the father, you probably have certain legal responsibilities, but I'm not about to start making demands. You know I don't need money. You asked if I was scared, and I guess if I am, it's only about this. I don't want fighting over this baby to ruin the friendship between us."

"I don't want that, either."

Mallory stepped back from him. "When do you have to get back to Ottawa?"

"I'm not sure. The Middle East story is out of the picture now, obviously. I was working on a piece about the foreign affairs minister, but I've finished my research and I have all my notes. It would be just as easy to write the story here as anywhere else."

"What about your radio show?"

"I was going to phone today and see if I could do that from the studio in Toronto."

"So you have a few days, then. To sort things out."

"At least. I was thinking of staying a couple of weeks, actually." Sorting out the tangle his mother's death had created would take at least that long. As for Mallory and the baby... It was too soon to know what impact they were going to have on his decisions.

DREW WAS VACUUMING his way up the wide central stairs, when Doug started to bark. Mallory had gone home about half an hour earlier, after they'd gotten the place almost back to normal. Drew turned off the power switch, and sure enough, seconds later he heard the knock.

Grady stood at the screen door in his jeans and an old plaid shirt. "Hey, buddy. I came to help clean up, but I see I'm a little late."

"That's okay. Mallory was here for a while." Drew checked the clock on the wall. It was well past noon. "Want something to eat? I've got about a dozen leftover casseroles you can choose from."

Grady brushed off his feet and followed Drew to the fridge.

"No, thanks. I just stopped over to have a coffee at Claire's and of course she had to make me lunch, even gave me a goodie bag to take home. Then I dropped in at the post office, and while I was there I heard something you might be interested in. But first I have to ask you—did you know Mallory's pregnant?"

Drew's hand paused over the tin of pop he'd taken out for himself. "I heard."

"Claire told me. I can hardly believe it. Claire says Mallory's happy and all, but I feel like I want to nail the guy who did it. She says it wasn't Randall, but I don't know. You never met him, did you?"

"Never had the pleasure." Drew leaned against the counter and took a long swallow. And hoped Grady didn't notice that his hand was shaking and he couldn't look him in the eye.

If the situation were reversed, he'd have felt exactly the same as Grady.

"Well, I did, and if you ask me, the only reason Mallory dated him was that she felt sorry for him. If this is the way he's chosen to repay her... Well, Mallory deserves better—I can tell you that much."

"No question," Drew agreed, taking another swallow.

"She's going to raise the baby on her own." Grady shrugged. Obviously he had his reservations. "I don't know... I suppose it's none of my business."

"It *is* Mallory's decision." As he said the words, though, a new thought hit him. Wasn't it his decision, too? He dismissed the idea. Mallory had this whole thing figured out, and unless he was prepared to offer something better, he'd best just step to the side and let her do what she wanted.

"Anyway," Grady continued, "the news I really

came to tell you was that one of the cottages along Cox Bay was broken into last night.''

Drew ran a hand over the top of his head. Cottages closed for the winter were always a target. Particularly for young teenagers with trouble on their minds.

"They catch the kids?" he asked.

Grady shook his head. ''No. But I thought you might want to check into it. For the paper.''

"Well, thanks.'' They chatted for a few minutes more, until Grady said he had to get home. Drew watched his friend leave, wondering what was going on. Why would anyone, particularly a good friend like Grady, assume that just because he'd put out one commemorative issue for his mother, he was planning to continue publishing the *Gazette?*

Drew set the empty soda tin on the kitchen counter and considered his options. If he printed another paper, a regular weekly edition, everybody would come to the same assumption Grady had made—that he was taking over from his mother.

On the other hand, since he'd be here for the next few weeks anyway, publishing the paper would give him something to do. Would leave less of that empty, thinking time he was trying so hard to avoid. Besides, reporting on school-board meetings and vandalized cottages could make for a nice change from wars and natural disasters.

It wouldn't hurt to check out the vandalized cottage. A drive in the country might be exactly what he needed right now. Maybe Mallory would like to come with him.

"IT'S OKAY, CLAIRE," Mallory said into the phone. "I don't mind that Grady knows. I guess it really is time to let other people in on it."

"Have you told Drew?"

"Yes. Last night." And what a disappointment that had been. The emotion had caught her unexpectedly, making her wonder if subconsciously she'd hoped for a different reception to her news. She and Drew had always been friends. Had she dreamed, on some level, that this baby might start Drew thinking of her as something more?

But that was preposterous. More than anyone else, she knew what Drew was like. Given the life-style he'd chosen, a traditional marriage with children was out of the question. And she was the last person to try to trap him into that.

She turned at the sound of tapping on the back window. "Speaking of the devil, he's at the door now." With her free hand she waved him inside.

"I'd better let you go then," Claire said. "I'll call you next week."

"Thanks. Have a safe drive back to Toronto."

"Hey, Mal." Car keys dangled from Drew's index finger, and she wondered what was up.

Just the sight of him standing there brought an

extra brightness to her kitchen. That grin, those mocking blue eyes. His tall slender build, the way he was slouching against the door frame reminded her of a poster she'd once seen of James Dean. Of course, Drew was older, but the two men shared that look of deceptive languor.

"Feel like a ride in the country? Grady says a cottage was vandalized. I thought I might investigate."

Mallory was surprised to hear that. Did he plan on writing a report for the *Gazette?* The only way the local paper would be printed next week was if he did it. When Drew had said he was planning to stay a couple of weeks, she hadn't thought he meant to carry on with the *Gazette.* "Does that mean what I think it does?"

"I don't know." Drew jingled the keys in his hand. "I guess I'm considering it."

"Okay," she said, trying to sound nonchalant. But the news had her insides sparkling like the Christmas lights she hung all over the store every November. Drew staying a few extra weeks, Drew putting out the next few issues of the *Gazette...* Was she incredibly optimistic to think this might lead somewhere?

Drew in Port Carling on a permanent basis. Maybe it wasn't as impossible as she'd once thought.

She followed Drew to his mother's truck and opened the door so Doug could get into the back.

"Seems weird to drive my mom's vehicle again," Drew said as he backed out of the garage. "It makes me feel like a kid. I keep expecting to hear her tell me not to go too fast, and to make sure and top up the tank before I come back home."

The cottage wasn't far from town. Drew drove north on Muskoka 7, then took the first left before Port Sandfield.

"Grady stopped by after you left," he said conversationally.

Remembering that Claire had told Grady she was pregnant, Mallory asked cautiously, "Really?"

"Yeah. He'd just had lunch with Claire. She happened to mention you were going to have a baby. He didn't seem to have any clue I was the father."

"No one knows about that part." She shifted in her seat and noticed Drew tighten his grip on the steering wheel.

"How do you feel about that?"

"What do you mean?"

He threw a glance her way, his eyes dipping to her waist, then up to her face once more. "You've grown up in this town. People will wonder..."

"So let them."

"Are you sure? That's a pretty big secret to have to keep."

What was he saying? That he wanted her to tell

people he was the father? Watching Drew watching the road, Mallory doubted it. Before she could ask him what he meant, he went on.

"I don't understand how you can be so calm about this, Mal. Frankly, I'm terrified." One quick look at his face told her that was true. "But I don't want you to feel you're in this alone. Even if you're against it, I plan to help financially."

Money. His answer disappointed her. She hadn't figured Drew for the kind of man who thought you could discharge your responsibilities with cold hard cash.

"I've been chewing over what you said. How I could be an uncle or a family friend to the baby…"

Mallory nodded, but silently she wondered, would Drew be happy doing that? Would the baby?

"I think we need to turn at this corner." Drew stopped the vehicle and unrolled his window to examine a motley collection of wooden signposts that identified the owners of the cottages down the road. "The Bentleys," he said finally. "I guess we go left."

"I've always wondered if two-parent families were overrated," he continued a second later, picking up their interrupted conversation. "Look at you—you only had your aunt Norma. And I just had Angie."

True. But all her life she'd mourned the loss of her parents. And she wasn't that certain Drew hadn't missed having a father more than he admitted. Of course, he'd had his grandpa for the first ten years.

"I'm sure you're right." She would never have made the decision to raise this child on her own if she hadn't thought herself capable of it. That didn't mean the situation was optimal.

The vandalized cottage sat at the end of the lane and was deserted. Obviously, the police had finished their investigation. Drew parked and let Doug out of the truck.

The cottage itself was unassuming, built with a barn-style roof, the pine boards stained dark brown, with tan trim around the window frames and door.

Mallory followed Drew as he walked around the small structure, peering through each window. Whoever had broken in hadn't done much damage. All she noticed was a missing windowpane at the back door. A piece of clear plastic was taped over the opening, which Drew peeled away to get a better look.

He stepped back so she could see. Inside, everything was neat and tidy, as far as she could tell. Ashes littered the fireplace, but other than that, the place appeared unlived-in.

"If teenagers had in fact broken in, they must have fled before they'd had a chance to do much partying," Drew said.

"Or maybe the culprits were a couple of young lovers needing a bit of privacy...."

"Possibly." Drew withdrew then, repositioning the tape on the window. At a snap of his fingers, Doug was by his side.

"Find anyone in those trees?" Drew queried.

Doug just ran ahead to the truck.

Drew held the passenger door open for Mallory. As she got in, she asked, "Well, what do you think? Are you going to write up a story for the *Gazette?*"

His expression was serious as he paused for a moment, thinking. "I really should stop in at the police station and see what the local constable has to say." He brushed a hand over the top of his head, then took a big breath.

"I guess that means yes?"

He nodded. "What the hell. A couple more issues won't kill me."

CHAPTER SEVEN

FRIDAY NIGHT MALLORY picked up the phone to call
Drew. They'd fallen into a routine of sharing pizza
and renting a video at the end of each work week,
and now that she was in her fourth month of pregnancy, her problems with nausea had subsided. Suddenly, anchovies and olives appealed to her again.

"I'll order the 'all dressed,'" she told Drew on
the phone. "You pick the movie."

"You always say that, then complain if I don't
choose a romantic comedy."

"We watched that political satire last week," she
reminded him.

"And you fell asleep halfway through. At least I
have the good manners to watch all the way through
your movies."

"That's because they're so interesting. Thanks,
you've proven my point." Mallory disconnected,
laughing, then dialed their favorite pizza place. She
ordered a large "all dressed," then looked to see if
she had cold beer in the fridge. Pity she couldn't
have the real stuff, but Drew had scrounged up some
nonalcoholic beer that tasted almost as good.

Drew beat the pizza by ten minutes. She popped the movie in the VCR, pleased to see he'd selected an old favorite—*Four Weddings and a Funeral.*

"Oh, this is so good. His sister is so funny. Do you remember—"

"I haven't seen it." Drew was on the sofa, legs stretched out to the coffee table. His dark hair was in disarray as usual, and she couldn't resist the urge to reach out and muss it further.

"How is this possible? Drew, you *must* have seen this movie."

He stood as the doorbell rang. "Trust me, I haven't." He paid for the pizza, then opened the cardboard box. The aroma of fresh-baked dough, melted cheese and spicy meat made Mallory feel ravenous.

"Boy, it's great to be able to eat again."

"Good. You've got some catching up to do after those first few months."

Drew put a pizza slice on a white paper napkin and passed it to her. She wondered if he'd noticed that she'd started to wear maternity clothes. Well, sort of maternity. Her waist had finally expanded a couple of inches, so she no longer fit into anything with a waistband. Today she was wearing leggings and an oversize sweater. As she ate, she smoothed the fabric over her belly, thinking she saw the beginning of a bulge there.

Immediately, she realized Drew was watching.

She felt the heat rise in her cheeks and reached for her cold beer.

"You're so cute," Drew teased pulling a strand of her hair.

"And you're making fun of me," she said, smoothing her sweater down. "But don't you think I'm starting to look pregnant?"

"I don't know about your stomach. Other body parts—yes. They're definitely expanding."

Oh, she knew what he meant by that. She'd already gone up one bra size and would soon need another. She jabbed him with her elbow. "Trust you to notice."

"I'm a man, Mallory. Of course I noticed."

He wasn't kidding. Mallory felt a jolt in the bottom of her stomach. A heart-stopping memory of his hands cupping her bare breasts in the amber glow from the fireplace at his cabin in the Gatineaus, had her face growing hot.

All of a sudden, she was aware of how close they were sitting—his arm pressed into her shoulder, their thighs within a hair's width of separation. He was looking at her with half-open eyes that seemed focused on her chin or maybe her mouth.

"Do you want another beer?" She jumped up from the sofa. "This pizza's really spicy, don't you think?"

IN DREW'S OPINION, not only the pizza was spicy. He dropped his head to the back of the sofa and closed his eyes. The left side of his body felt cool with her gone, but his mind still steamed with the impulses he'd had when she'd sat next to him.

That response was becoming a real problem for him. Since he'd come home, he'd found himself growing more and more aware of Mallory, in a completely nonsisterly way. Like just now, when her face had been so near he could count her freckles. He wondered why, in all their years of friendship, he'd never really noticed her lips before. They were a pale-apricot color, soft and inviting and utterly kissable.

Kissable. There was a danger signal if ever he'd seen one. How could he think this way about Mallory? Was it because they'd made love that one time? Or was it because she was carrying his baby?

Did men usually find stuff like that erotic?

"I'm glad you've been able to prolong your stay, Drew. It's been great having you here." Mallory was back with two fresh beer cans.

He accepted one, welcoming the cold slick feel of the aluminum in his hands, tempted to press it to his forehead to cool himself down even further.

"It's been a nice change of pace for me, too," he admitted. Although it still burned a little whenever he read the news from the Middle East that continued to dominate the front page of the *Globe* and that should be running under his byline.

Mallory put a few feet between them this time when she sat down and an emotion as thick as Weber's chocolate milk shakes suddenly lodged in his throat.

What he'd said had been true—so far he was enjoying his time in Port Carling. Putting out the paper was more demanding than he'd expected, but he still had plenty of time to do the prep work for his weekly radio program. Driving into Toronto for recordings had turned out to be no problem.

In fact, nothing was a problem. He'd phoned the teenage boy in Ottawa who usually watched his place when he was out of town, and told him he'd be gone until after Christmas. Then he'd finished the story he'd been working on and faxed it to the *Ottawa Citizen*. A couple more phone calls, a bit of juggling with a colleague of his, and his schedule was clear. He'd never thought it would be that easy.

Maybe it was *too* easy.

After all, he had a life back in Ottawa. A downtown office, a house he loved. He had a bustling work schedule, and a growing reputation for fearless reporting and determined interviewing. There were colleagues and friends, though none he would put in the same category as Mallory, Grady and Claire.

On the TV screen the main male character was

chatting up the main female character, but Drew didn't have a clue what was going on. He wondered if Mallory's concentration was any better. She kept shifting positions, as though she couldn't get comfortable.

In the old days, she might have stretched out on the couch and put her feet on his lap. Somehow he knew she wouldn't tonight.

What was happening to them?

THE FIRST SUNDAY in November, Drew went to Mallory's shop with her to help decorate for Christmas. Mallory's carried upper-end sports clothing for women, as well as designer fashions for children from newborns to size fourteen. In addition, she stocked selected home-fashion items such as candles and picture frames.

Come Christmas, Mallory always did the store up big, with a holiday scene in the front window and fairy lights strung everywhere. He didn't want her lugging boxes and standing on ladders, even though she seemed to think it was no big deal.

"Where do you want this holly?" he asked. He was on the top rung of her stepladder, holding the wire gingerly. The holly was fresh and pricked him whenever he shifted it in his hands.

"Around the top of the doorway. In a sort of arch." Mallory strained her head back to watch. Her hair was loosely braided down her back, but it had puffed up around her face, and a couple of strands had broken free.

Drew attached the holly with staples, trying to do it the way Mallory had instructed. She thought of everything when she decorated the store, even the scent of the place. Earlier, she'd put some kind of fragrant oil into a little holder that sat on top of the lamp on the counter. Now the place smelled like Marg's Pastry Shop after she'd baked her traditional Christmas gingerbread men.

"What next?" He climbed down the ladder and looked up at his handiwork. The holly framed the entranceway nicely, emphasized by the string of fairy lights he'd hung earlier. Not bad at all.

"I think we're almost done." Mallory adjusted the hat on a teddy bear she had dressed in Victorian garb and posed by the store Christmas tree.

"Great, 'cause I'm starved. How about I run over to Marg's and get us something to eat?"

"I'll put the kettle on for herbal tea."

Herbal tea again. Fortunately, Marg made a very fine take-out coffee. He would get a large cup along with some food. Marg's shop was only a few doors down from Mallory's, but the walk over was long enough for him to feel the nip in the air and to notice the low clouds overhead. He guessed Port Carling's first snowfall of the season was about to start any minute.

Mallory was sitting in the love seat in the back room of the store when he returned. She had her mug of tea in her hands, and her feet were propped up on the wicker table in front of her.

He passed her a sandwich, then unwrapped his own.

"This is good," she admitted a few minutes later. "I guess I was hungrier than I thought."

"Me, too." He'd devoured his roast-beef-and-cheddar sub. Now he glanced over at Mallory, his attention caught by her thickening middle. She was eighteen weeks. He'd have thought she'd be much bigger, but she said her size was normal.

"It's because I'm tall and this is my first baby."

He supposed that if her doctor was happy, he himself shouldn't worry. What did he know about pregnancy? He trashed the remains of his lunch and was about to start on his coffee, when he realized Mallory's face had gone still and her hand was brushing her tummy.

"What is it, Mal?"

"I just felt something move. Inside me." She cocked her head, concentrating on the message from her body.

"Really?"

"Come." She tapped the space beside her. "Put your hand here."

He did, but couldn't feel a thing beyond the warmth of her body and the soft weave of her sweater.

"Maybe I imagined it," Mallory said after a few minutes. "It was very faint."

Drew stroked her belly through the silky knit sweater. "What did it feel like?" He could smell her perfume, subtle and sweet, and became aware that he wanted to put his arm around her and pull her close to him.

Protective. That was what he was feeling. Natural enough, under the circumstances.

"It felt like tinsel paper blowing in a breeze."

Drew tried to imagine something moving inside him but couldn't. "If you keep feeling things like that, I'm going to start thinking you have a baby in there." He patted her stomach.

"That's the idea." She turned to him. "It still doesn't seem real to you, does it?"

"Real enough." Seeing Mallory's body change had done it. And not just because of her waistline. Her breasts had continued to swell over the weeks he'd been home. And more than once he'd fantasized about what they would look like naked. He just couldn't stop himself, no matter how much he tried. What worried him most was that Mallory would guess what he was thinking. Even now she was eyeing him most peculiarly—

A knock at the front door had him glancing back into the store. "Expecting someone?"

"Hardly." She shook a few crumbs off her sweater, then went to investigate. A moment later she came back with Grady.

"I saw Angie's Explorer in front," Grady said. "Figured you guys would be here."

"What's up?"

"Bess was out so I went in to work on an antique boat for a customer of mine—floorboards are completely rotted. Then I decided I needed a break. Would you like to go for a coffee or something?"

"Drew just had one," Mallory said. "I could make you some tea, though. The water just boiled."

"Sure." Grady paced the distance from the microwave to the sink. "Place looks good. All ready for Christmas, then?"

"You bet." Mallory plugged in the kettle. "What's wrong, Grady? You seem ready to spit nails."

"Ah. It's my boys." He picked a mug out of the cupboard, then grabbed a tea bag from a canister near the sink.

Drew couldn't help but think how at home Grady appeared here. Well, why not? He had been friends with Mallory as long as Drew had. And he hadn't spent the past ten years living in a different city.

"What have Warren and Taylor been up to now?"

"It's pretty serious this time." Grady's light-blue eyes traveled from one friend to the next. "They took my Jeep last night."

"Your Jeep?" Drew asked. "But they're only fifteen. They can't have their driver's licenses yet."

"You've got that right."

Mallory poured boiling water into Grady's mug, her gaze flickering anxiously from Drew to Grady.

"Bess and I drove over to Bracebridge in her car to visit friends yesterday evening. We came home earlier than expected because…because Bess wasn't feeling that great. When we pulled into the garage, the Jeep was missing. And the boys were nowhere to be found."

"What did you do?"

Grady sat down, bowing his head. "Didn't know what to do. Phone the police on my own boys? Maybe I should have. Bess wanted me to. But the kids showed up fifteen minutes later."

"Any damage?"

"Nope. Thank goodness. Anyway, the boys are grounded until Christmas, though I don't know that it'll do any good. Neither one has spoken a word to me or their mother."

"I don't get it. I realize I haven't spent much time with them lately, but Warren and Taylor are good kids. Wasn't it two summers ago that we took them backpacking for a weekend? They were such troupers, not a word of complaint."

"Yeah, Drew. They were thirteen then. The past couple of years have made a big difference. Plus a new kid moved into town last year, and I don't think he's such a great influence. He's a year older than the twins, and I've heard he smokes and drinks. The boys claim they're not doing any of that. I can only hope they're telling the truth."

"Jeez, Grady. Is there anything we can do?"

"I'm glad you asked." Grady eyed at him frankly. "I'd appreciate it if you'd try talking to them. Maybe, since you're not their old man, they'd listen to you. I know they've always looked up to you."

Drew crossed his arms. "Are you sure you're asking the right person? You and I did some pretty wild things when we were that age, as I recall."

"Maybe. But we never stole anything."

He had a point there. "Well, I can give it a shot, I suppose. But you know I don't have much experience with kids." He glanced at Mallory, and could tell she was thinking the same thing he was. Yet.

Once Grady had finished his tea and left, Mallory started to pull on her coat, brown suede with a thick pile lining. "Will you drop me home before you go talk to Warren and Taylor?"

"Of course. But wait one minute."

He'd put a hand on her arm, and she peered at it for a moment before turning her gaze to his. "What's up?"

"I got word this morning that another cottage was broken into last night. Not five miles from the last one. What do you think?"

She was quiet for a few seconds. "Do you think the boys might have had something to do with it?"

"I don't know. I hope not."

Still, it was quite a coincidence.

CHAPTER EIGHT

GRADY AND BESS HOGAN'S house was nestled against the Indian River, which connected Port Carling with the three great Muskoka lakes: Rosseau, Muskoka and Joseph. A sprawling bungalow, with pale-gray cedar siding, it had a double garage out front and a boathouse at the back, connected to the house by a long, freshly painted dock.

Drew found the twins in the boathouse. They were cleaning the small motorboat the family used for touring. The larger craft, with enough horsepower for waterskiing, had already been pulled out of the water and was hidden from view by a large canvas cover.

"Hey, guys," Drew said as he ducked through the small door. The boathouse provided shelter from the wind and from the snow, which had only just begun to fall. But it was still cool inside. Drew zipped up his leather jacket and pushed his hands into the warmth of the lined pockets.

The boys were wearing jeans and sweatshirts, their coats tossed on the ground beside them. Taylor was wiping the interior of the boat with a rag, while

Warren worked with sandpaper on a couple of deep scratches.

Although the twins were identical, Drew had no trouble distinguishing them. Mostly it was personality. You could just see that Warren was the live wire, whereas Taylor had a quieter disposition, reflected in the evenness of his expression.

He crouched down to their level and picked up a rag. "I heard you weren't speaking to your folks. Not talking to me, either?"

Taylor had the grace to look at him sheepishly. But a glance from Warren had Taylor's eyes focused back on the boat.

"I guess you figure I'm here to give you hell, and you're not interested."

"We don't care why you're here," Warren said, still sanding with long even strokes.

"You don't, do you? Well, that kind of hurts my feelings, because I thought we were friends. Remember who it was who stood in the water for an hour straight, helping you two get up your first time on skis? It was only June and the water was freezing cold as I recall."

"It wasn't an hour," Taylor protested. "We both got up on practically our first try."

"I believe your mother's got some serious video footage that will prove you wrong."

Taylor ducked his head, hiding a smile. That was a good sign.

"So what sports are you guys into these days? Still playing hockey?"

"Nah. We dropped out of that last year. We've got better things to do with our time." This came from Warren, who'd always been the more competitive athlete.

Drew didn't think the boy was talking about studying. "Like what?"

"Hanging out with our friends."

"You mean the guys you were with when you stole your dad's Jeep last night?"

Warren's gaze flashed to his brother. "See. I told you he was here to give us the big lecture."

Drew surmised they must have seen him drive up to the house, then made sure they were busy when he walked in the door.

"That's where you're wrong, Warren. I have no big lecture. Just questions. Your dad came to see me this morning to tell me what happened last night. He's real worried about the two of you, and so am I.

"It just doesn't make sense. You're bright kids. You know the trouble you could get into driving without a license. I can't believe you'd be that dumb. I figure someone else was driving. One of those friends you were talking about."

The boys exchanged another look, and he concluded he was right. Was it this new kid Grady seemed so worried about?

"Of course, this hypothetical friend of yours couldn't have done it unless you guys gave him the keys. Which is bad enough. I'm just hoping that a bit of back-road driving is all that went on. That there was no drinking or..." He paused for a moment, assessing their faces. "Breaking into any of the cottages closed up for the winter."

"Why would you say that?" Warren asked quickly. "Are you accusing us of something?"

"I'm not accusing you of anything. I'm just trying to warn you. I was listening to the scanner this morning. Seems another cottage was vandalized last night. The same night you and your brother were out driving in your father's Jeep without permission. And maybe without a legal driver, either. People can and will put two and two together."

He stood, brushing dirt off his jeans. "Now, I'm not saying there's any connection. But if there is, the consequences will be a lot scarier than being grounded for a month. And your mom and dad won't be able to help you."

"As if they'd want to," Warren said, tossing the sandpaper to the side. "Mom's ready to have us locked in jail already. We wouldn't be such a nuisance to her that way."

Whoa. Where had that come from? "Is there some problem with your mom these days?"

"Maybe you should ask her that. We don't see her enough to know. Neither does Dad. Maybe you should ask him, too. Maybe you should do a complete bloody report on the entire family. That might turn up a few interesting facts for the *Gazette*."

The teen's anger stung Drew into a silence that was long enough for Warren to storm out of the boathouse, followed rapidly by Taylor.

Drew felt helpless watching them go. He thought he'd driven up here to deal with a little teenage rebellion. But this anger toward Bess—where had it come from? Did Grady have any idea of the hornet's nest he'd asked his friend to stir up?

DREW WAS SHOVELING her walk when Mallory opened her front door Monday morning. The unpleasant sound of metal scraping concrete echoed in the still air. A heavy snow had fallen all night, wet and sticky, perfect for…

She bent down, feeling a little guilty. The guy was clearing her driveway, for heaven's sake. Yet the temptation was too strong.

Splat! She got him on the side of the neck. She'd always had pretty good aim. He straightened, his hand coming up to where she'd hit him, then slowly he faced her.

"Good morning," she said sweetly. And shut the door.

Ten minutes later, there was a knock at the back. She already had her coat and boots on and was about to leave for work. Cautiously, Mallory inched open

the door. Sure enough, there stood Drew, his dark
hair on end, his cheeks ruddy with cold.

"Want a ride to the store?" he offered.

He sounded so polite. But she wasn't fooled. His
gem-blue eyes sparkled, and one hand was behind
his back.

"No, thanks." She tried to shut the door, but he'd
wedged in the toe of his hiking boot.

"No, Drew!" she shrieked as he grabbed her arm.
A moment later her face was coated with frosty, wet
mush. She sputtered for air, bent at the waist, then
clutched at the snow by her feet. She hardly had
time to throw it in his direction, when he hit her
again, this time with a soft ball aimed at the back
of her head.

"You're lucky I don't wear makeup, or you'd be
in big trouble right now." She had two snowballs
in her hands, and he was unarmed. She stalked him
through the yard until he was backed up against the
garage.

"This is going to be fun." She raised her arm,
aiming right for his face, then he lunged, and they
were both on the ground. He cushioned her fall with
his body, though, bringing her down gently. Then
he swung her over and planted another handful of
snow in her face.

"Ungrateful wretch. Shovel your own walks next
time."

Mallory's lashes were heavy with moisture, and

her cheeks burned with the fresh bite of the snow crystals. "You expect a poor pregnant woman to shovel her own walks?" She let her voice whine with self-pity.

Drew blinked. She could see the beads of water on the tips of his dark lashes and along the ends of his hair. Poor guy, he looked even more disheveled than usual.

"You *are* okay, aren't you?"

She laughed to reassure him, realizing she should have known better than to tease. He was so paranoid about her pregnancy he didn't think she ought to do anything remotely physical. Her doctor had assured her, however, that she could carry on with all her usual activities.

"I'm fine. A little damp, but fine." That was when she became aware of the intimacy of their situation. She was still half on Drew's body, her left leg between his, her head propped up by his hand. His breath warmed the tip of her nose; his mouth was only inches from her own.

Suddenly, it hurt to breathe, and she felt a twisting and tumbling in her stomach that had nothing to do with the baby inside her. Drew's eyes had grown serious, and his mouth had gone still. She and Drew were having another one of those moments that seemed to now occur with increasing frequency. It was almost like a spell had been cast over them, which inevitably one or the other of them would break. This morning it was Drew.

"You'll dry." He pulled away from her, dragged himself out of the snow, then held out his hand.

"Yes, I suppose I will." She let him pull her up, focusing on the roll of his black turtleneck, rather than his face.

A little melted snow wasn't the problem here. For a moment there, she'd thought he was going to kiss her—and she had so badly wanted him to—

"Drew."

He'd been walking ahead of her. Now he glanced at her from over his shoulder. "I'd better get you to the store or the customers are going to be lined up for blocks."

"Yeah, right." She'd be lucky to have one customer show on a snowy Monday morning in November. But that wasn't the point. What Drew was really saying was that he didn't want to talk about what had happened in that snowy bank.

How long could they go on pretending that nothing was changed between them?

TURNED OUT SHE DID get a customer, though not the kind she expected would buy anything. Around eleven, a petite woman with striking black hair, a full generous mouth and large, haunting eyes came, young daughter in tow. They were both dressed poorly for the weather. The woman's jeans had a tear in the right knee, and her sweater, while thick, was no barrier to the low temperature and blowing wet snow.

The tiny child holding her hand had little better. Her ski jacket was colorless and thin from too many washings. The hat that covered most of her hair—dark like her mom's—was too big for her head and kept falling over her eyes.

"Good morning," Mallory said cheerfully. She walked around the counter, where she'd been counting off her order sheets, and held out a bowl to the little girl.

"Would it be okay if your daughter had some of these candies?" she asked the mother.

The woman looked anxious at first, then she smiled. "Thank you. That would be very nice. What do you say, Lisa?"

The little girl couldn't have been more than three. She reached into the bowl of cellophane-wrapped peppermints and took one, lisping slightly when she said, "Thank you."

"Grab a handful," Mallory urged. "You, too." She smiled at the mother.

The woman just shook her head. "No, thanks."

"Well, feel free to look around as long as you like." Mallory stepped behind the counter again, giving them space. The woman led her daughter to the back, where a new shipment of little girls' woolen coats, accompanied by fluffy white muffs, was hanging.

"Aren't those darling? Just like something out of *Little Women*," Mallory said.

The woman withdrew her hand and moved farther back to a rack where two-piece snowsuits were marked down ten percent. The reduction, however, still brought them nowhere near the price you'd pay for an equally warm—admittedly not as fashionable—outfit at a larger discount store.

"These are so cute," the woman said, holding out a hanger with a dark-red snowsuit. "This color would look perfect on you, Lisa. Too bad I can't afford it." She replaced it on the rack and smiled back at Mallory.

"Are you new to the area?" Mallory asked. At this time of the year they had few tourists, especially during the week. But she couldn't recall having seen this woman or her child before.

The question, meant to be friendly, seemed to make the woman apprehensive.

"Yes. Relatively new. We used to live in Toronto."

"With my daddy," piped up the little girl, pushing the hat up from her eyes so she had a clear view of Mallory.

The woman glanced down at her daughter, then flashed a nervous smile at Mallory. "We've recently separated."

That explained the pain in the woman's dark eyes.

"I'm Mallory Lombard. I've lived in Port Carling all my life. My house is on Bailey Street."

"Terese Mer—. No, Terese Balfour." She gave a disparaging shrug. "I've gone back to my maiden name."

Again, she appeared to flinch, almost as if afraid. Or maybe she was just shy. It was a shame. There was something about this woman that made Mallory think they could be friends. And if Terese had just moved to a new place and left her husband, she could probably stand to make a few new friends.

"As you can tell, business is really slow right now. Would you like to stay for a minute and have a cup of coffee? I think I have juice in the fridge for your daughter."

"Oh, that's so kind of you. But you're busy."

"I wish." Mallory laughed. "Look, the door has a bell, so I'll hear if anyone comes in. Why don't you keep me company while I take a break."

"Well, when you put it that way…" Terese took her daughter's hand and followed Mallory to the back room.

Mallory had put on a pot of decaf coffee earlier in the morning. She poured her guest a mug, dug out the bran muffin and apple she'd brought for her lunch, cut them into pieces and arranged them on a plate. "Help yourself," she said while she poured Lisa's juice.

Lisa spared one questioning glance at her mother, before her little hand reached out for a piece of the muffin. A minute later she had gobbled down two slices of apple.

"That's enough, sweetheart," Terese said. "Leave some for everyone else."

"But no one else is eating," Lisa pointed out.

Mallory was amused. "You go ahead, Lisa. I'm not very hungry right now." In fact she was starving, and she hoped her stomach didn't betray her and start growling. But once Terese and her daughter left she could duck over to Marg's and grab a sandwich. She had a feeling food, as well as warm clothing, was in short supply with the two.

"So what do you do?" she asked Terese.

"Before I had Lisa, I was a high-school guidance counselor, but what I really love is painting. Mostly landscapes and the occasional still life."

"That sounds fascinating. I wish I had a talent like that."

Out of the blue, Lisa spoke, her mouth full of muffin. "My daddy hits me. My daddy is bad."

"Lisa!" Terese's mug landed on the table with a thud.

The little girl stopped chewing.

"Sweetheart," Terese continued in a softer tone, "don't talk with your mouth full, okay? Now, finish your juice."

She glanced at Mallory, then back to her hands, which were clasped on her·lap.

"I'm sorry. We should be going. We've kept you too long."

"No, you haven't."

But Terese was already zipping her little girl's coat and slipping the too-big hat back on the child's head.

Mallory wanted to stop her, to tell her that if she needed a favor, all she had to do was ask. But Terese had whisked her daughter out of the store. Mallory listened to the bells tinkle as they left, wondering if what the little girl had said was true.

In her experience children could be both frightfully honest and imaginatively inventive with the stories they told to adults. She had no idea which it was in this case, although an abusive husband certainly would help explain that sad, almost fearful expression in Terese Balfour's eyes.

All day long Mallory kept thinking of that look and the matter-of-fact tone of Lisa's voice: "My daddy hits me." She could have been saying, "My daddy's an accountant," for all the emotion she'd displayed. But that didn't necessarily mean it hadn't happened.

How often had he hit her?

It was none of her business, Mallory told herself. Still she was worried. She couldn't help but place herself in Terese's shoes and wonder how she would cope if the situation were reversed.

Around closing time the truth hit her. In about three years she would be in Terese's situation. A young mother raising her child on her own.

And what about Drew? Would he be in the picture? Or just a name scrawled on the bottom of monthly support checks?

CHAPTER NINE

SINCE THANKSGIVING, Buddy Conroy's workdays seemed to have lengthened, and his enthusiasm for his profession waned. Now, on this early December evening, Buddy felt more tired than usual, and oddly dispirited. With one hand on the steering wheel, he navigated the familiar streets of Port Carling, musing that maybe the time had come to consider retiring. There were other good lawyers in the area, even if he was the only one in Port Carling. He was curious what Patricia would think of the idea.

Buddy's foot hit the brake as he drove past Angie's house. Twisting his arm to the right, he pulled over to the side of the road.

Didn't the place look just like old times. Drew must have put up every one of his mother's Christmas lights. Angie had always gone in for the holidays in a big way. That included decorating her house with lights along the roofline, the railing of the veranda, and all over the two columnar cedars that stood on either side of the steps leading to the front door.

Then there was her annual Christmas Eve mid-

night buffet, held after the candlelight church service. No one minded that the food was all reheated
prepared dishes bought in bulk at one of those discount warehouses in Toronto. Companionship and
good cheer—and the hostess, always stunning in her
long velvet skirt and satin blouse—drew the towns-
people in for a cup of mulled wine or a glass of
homemade brandy.

Conversations at those parties were always something to remember. Angie had a way of sparking
controversy with a single question or an aptly
worded comment. She brought out retiring person-
alities and invigorated those individuals who were
more outgoing.

Life. Spirit. Acumen.

That had been Angie.

What was Christmas going to be like without her?

At least his own children, Laura and Robert, were
coming home, Laura from university in Kingston,
and Robert and his wife from Toronto.

That made Buddy think of Drew, who'd extended
his stay much longer than anyone had expected. He
was still doing his radio program but had temporar-
ily put his freelance work on hold. That was what
he told everyone.

But Buddy wondered. Was the traveling man finally settling down? To have a Driscoll living in this
house, to have the *Hub of the Lakes Gazette* con-

tinue in this town, would be good things, Buddy decided. Good for all of them, including Drew.

If that was what Angie's son wanted. Buddy wished he could believe it was.

But there was still something unsettled about that boy. Buddy felt a stirring of anxiety every time he saw him. Drew was not a man at peace, and it showed in little ways. His constant activity, the way his eyes never remained on anything, or anyone, for too long.

He was struggling, and Buddy wished that he himself were in a position to help. With Angie gone, he felt responsible.

But what could he do? He had so little maneuvering room. Just watch, and hope and pray that the boy would figure things out on his own? That didn't seem enough. Not for Angie or Drew, and especially not for himself.

His sense of dissatisfaction even greater than before, Buddy pulled back into the street to drive home for dinner.

"DREW, COULD YOU SET the table while I mash the potatoes?"

Mallory had invited Claire and the girls for dinner. School was out for the holidays and the Ridgeways were in Port Carling for the festive season, with Kirk to follow in about a week, on Christmas Eve.

Mallory had chosen the menu carefully: mashed potatoes for Andie; creamed corn, which was Jenna's favorite; and Shake 'n Bake chicken, for Daisy.

Hardly the gourmet fare Claire would have served, but hers was a standard Mallory didn't even attempt to measure up to.

Certainly the girls appeared to enjoy the meal. And Claire polished off her plate quickly. "It's such a treat not to cook for a change."

"Yummy," Daisy said, then asked for seconds of everything.

"Sure thing, sweetie," Mallory said.

Across the table, Drew looked amused. "Mallory has a way with creamed corn, don't you think?"

"It's all in how you open the can," Mallory said. "Although I really shouldn't be sharing my secrets like this. Before you know it, Jenna'll think just anyone can make creamed corn."

"Not this good." Jenna was staunchly loyal.

"No wonder I love you kids so much." A familiar warmth stole into Mallory's heart. Nothing meant more to her than moments like these, when she was surrounded by her oldest and dearest friends.

Only now, the knowledge that next yuletide season her own baby would be on the scene intensified the feeling. Her little girl would be around eight months old, and sitting for sure. Maybe crawling.

Mallory imagined tiny feet in sleepers, disappearing around the corner into the living room. And smiled.

"You look happy," Drew murmured as he brushed behind her to gather her plate. She felt the touch of his arm, the press of his chest with an awareness that was becoming all too familiar.

"I *am* happy," she said, but his comment had reminded her of the one problem in her life. Their relationship. She just hoped they could sort everything out before the baby arrived.

"Anyone interested in seeing the Magic School Bus explore the solar system?" Drew asked, interrupting her reverie.

It was a new computer game he'd picked up on his last trip to Toronto, and was supposedly a Christmas gift, although it figured he couldn't wait to show it to the girls. He winked at Claire and Mallory as the three girls jumped out of their chairs.

"I'll bring them back in an hour or so."

Once they were gone, Mallory surveyed the messy table and came to a decision. "Let's leave the dishes and take our tea to the living room." They both had needlework projects—hers was a cross-stitch for the baby's room; Claire's was a tree skirt she hoped to finish before Christmas.

"You and Drew seem awfully cozy," Claire commented once she'd organized her sewing.

"I suppose." Mallory bent over her paper pattern, feeling the backs of her ears burn. Had Claire guessed Drew was the baby's father? She didn't want to give anything away by letting her friend see her expression. "It's like old times having him next door again."

"I'll bet."

"Claire!"

"Well, why else is he staying so long? It's been over two months since Angie died."

Mallory threaded a needle with a double strand of lavender floss. "Yes, but he's had so much to sort out. The house, the paper..." *The baby.* She pulled the needle carefully up through one tiny hole until the thread was taut. "I thought that was obvious."

"Drew wouldn't give up his big-time career to run the *Hub of the Lakes Gazette.* I figure it has to be you he's staying for."

If only. Mallory quashed the foolish hope. "I don't think he's made any decisions. At least not yet." Mallory knew it was selfish of her to be glad about that, but she was. The longer Drew postponed his decision, the longer he would be around.

"My eyes hurt." Claire set down her project and went to the front window. "Looks like we're getting more snow."

"As if we don't have enough already." Above-average snowfalls had enveloped Port Carling this winter. In Mallory's yard snowbanks buried all but her tallest shrubs, and at least four feet of the white stuff had drifted against the north side of her house.

"How have you kept up with all the shoveling?"

"Drew's done most of it."

"Really?"

Mallory counted stitches carefully, aware that Claire was observing her.

"Are you sure there isn't something going on between the two of you?"

Ouch. Mallory looked at the tip of her finger, where a dot of blood sat like a tiny ball. She put down the linen fabric and reached for a tissue. "Why would you ask a crazy question like that?"

"What's so crazy about it?"

"Well, we're talking about Drew, for one thing. We used to take baths together, for heaven's sake."

"Sounds good to me."

Mallory withdrew the tissue and checked her finger. Once more the blood began to pool. She replaced the tissue and pressed hard. "And I'm pregnant. Not the best time to start a romance."

"Depends how you view it. In some respects, it's the perfect time."

"Drew has enough on his plate right now. Besides, he's never thought of me that way—romantically, I mean." Maybe *never* might be stretching the truth. They had conceived a baby together, after all.

But it hadn't been planned. It had been a mistake. Hadn't he said so himself? As for those electric little moments that had started sparking between the two of them—well, he seemed determined that they wouldn't lead anywhere.

Besides, eventually the changes to her body were sure to repulse him. She was more than twenty weeks pregnant, and her condition was now obvious, even to strangers. Soon her waist measurement would be bigger than her bust. Then how would she compare with the svelte beauties she knew he preferred?

She was content, though. Nothing made her happier than to feel how her stomach rounded out in front of her. Yet she could hardly expect a man to appreciate her new, generous shape. Especially a man who'd been with as many pretty women as Drew had. And who'd never intended, or wished, to become a father.

If only she could harness her attraction toward him. But ever since he'd come home, Drew was no longer just a friend to her. He was a man. And when they were together, she couldn't forget it. Not for a moment.

He'd be uncomfortable if he knew how often she thought of that weekend they'd made love. He'd be mortified if he knew that she secretly wished it could happen again.

Fat chance of that.

"Feelings can change, Mallory. You know, evolve. Just because Drew hasn't thought of you in that way before doesn't mean it isn't possible."

Mallory sucked in a deep breath, thinking how wonderful these past few months had been, and how much better they would be if... If.

"Claire, forget evolution. It would take a *revolution* for Drew's feelings for me to change that much. I'm his buddy. His friend. His *pregnant* friend."

"Pregnancy can be a turn-on for some men."

"You've got to be kidding." Seeing Claire's smile, Mallory had to grin, too. "You mean Kirk—"

"Oh, yeah." Claire's smile widened, and she went to the tree that Mallory had decorated with tiny teddy bears from the store. She fingered one of the delicate stuffed creatures. "Maybe I should get pregnant again...."

The smile was gone, and that lost look Mallory had glimpsed at Thanksgiving was in its place.

"What's wrong, Claire? Is there a problem between you and Kirk?"

"Things aren't perfect right now." Claire shook her head, compressing her lips. "But what marriage ever is?"

Mallory had always thought Claire and Kirk's came pretty darn close. "Is it his work?"

Claire nodded. "He's away so much. And when he finally does get home, he's often distracted. Sometimes I don't think he even sees us anymore."

"You two need a long weekend away together. I'll watch the girls for you. You know I'd love to."

"He'd never take the time off work."

"You could ask him."

"I suppose." Claire let go of the bear. "But first we have to survive Christmas."

Since when was Christmas something you had to survive? Claire had always loved the holiday as much as Mallory. They both enjoyed crafts, and Claire went overboard with her baking....

Disquiet pushed aside the warm contentment she'd felt earlier. Determined, she started up with her stitching again. "Have you told Grady you're back?"

"I called him before we came here. He's not happy, either, Mallory. Do you know what's going on?"

"Not really. There're some problems with the twins." Oh, how she hoped they weren't responsible for the recent cottage break-ins. She didn't see how they could be. Basically, they were good kids.

"What about Bess?" Claire asked bluntly.

"Well, she's certainly been acting strange lately. It seems she's never home anymore—she's out most evenings. Sometimes Grady goes with her, but often she's alone. There's probably a good reason...."

She and Drew had discussed the situation. He'd told her what happened when he tried to talk to the twins the month before. Since then, he'd made a couple of other attempts to get the boys to spend some time with him, but they remained withdrawn.

"It isn't fair," Claire said. "Grady's such a sweetheart."

Mallory couldn't argue with that. Grady was the kind of guy who always stopped if he saw someone in trouble. In school, he'd gotten into more fights sticking up for the underdog. He'd only been eighteen when he and Bess had had the twins; some men might have resented the early responsibility, but Mallory had never seen a more devoted father.

"I'm sure they'll work this out," she said, but she didn't feel any corresponding certainty in her heart.

The truth was, her friends' problems were frightening her. For years she'd looked at Grady and Bess and the boys, and Claire and Kirk and the girls, and considered them the luckiest people on earth.

Perhaps she'd idealized their lives somewhat. Maybe the flaws had always been there and she just hadn't seen them.

Until her pregnancy. Now she was about to become a parent, too. She and this baby—they would be a family.

Usually, that thought delighted her. But suddenly, she wondered, if two-parent families were having trouble, how much harder would it be for her?

And for her baby.

MISTLETOE HUNG OVER THE front door, and Drew kissed his guests as they came in out of the cold. The female ones, anyway.

It was Christmas Eve, and he was holding the Driscolls' traditional open house, with all the trimmings, just as his mother would have and her mother before her. Including mulled wine, Christmas carols, packaged appetizers...

And mistletoe.

"Mallory." Drew swallowed as his next-door neighbor, and best friend, appeared at the door. In her dark-brown cashmere coat, you couldn't tell she was pregnant. But you could see that she was beautiful.

For once her hair was down, a riot of curls dusted by flakes of white snow. Her skin glowed with health, and her green eyes danced the way they always did when she was happy.

She'd spent the afternoon at his place, helping him set out food on trays and making sure they had enough ice cubes, and napkins for all the finger food. Then they'd attended the Christmas Eve service together, after which she'd gone home for a moment to freshen up. This had been less than an hour ago.

So why did he feel that glad now to see her? As if it had been weeks, or even months. He already had things to tell her, and the party had only started.

"Mistletoe, Drew?" She glanced up, obviously amused.

"It *is* a tradition." And didn't it provide the perfect opportunity for just one little kiss…?

He lowered his head, and her lips as they brushed his were warm and soft, but her cheek was cold. Taking in a gulp of winter air, he put an arm around her waist, tempted to draw her closer. To kiss her again. A real kiss this time, the kind he had no business wanting as desperately as he did.

But he stood back.

"Let me hang your coat." He held on to the collar as she withdrew first one arm, then the other. Now, outlined in the soft cotton of her tunic top, he could see the bulge at her middle, the lushness of her breasts. He felt a familiar ache—starting in his chest and moving down to settle in his groin—and kept his hands firmly on her coat.

"There's hot apple cider in the kitchen," he told her.

"I can smell it from here."

He drew a deep breath, taking in not the aroma of cinnamon and apples but the tantalizing scent of what he was sure was her new perfume; she hadn't been wearing this fragance at church earlier in the evening. "You look great, Mal. You smell good, too."

"I stole a few things from the latest shipment," she confessed.

He'd only just shut the door, but now the bell chimed again.

"Help yourself to the cider?"

"I will." She turned and disappeared into the crowd.

At least thirty people had already arrived, and more were still coming. Drew opened the door to find Buddy and Patricia Conroy stomping snow from their boots.

"Come in. Merry Christmas." Drew gave Patricia a peck on the cheek and shook Buddy's hand.

"Glad you're keeping up your mother's traditions," Buddy said warmly. "I know she would have been real happy."

Drew shut the door, and this time managed to get his guests settled with a glass of mulled wine before the bell rang again. It was Grady. Without Bess or the boys.

"Hey, pal, come on in." Drew clasped his shoulder and practically pulled him through the door. He saw the apology in his friend's eyes, and felt a stab of sorrow. No wife and no boys. Seeing Grady on his own these days was becoming more and more common.

But Christmas Eve?

Couldn't Bess have made an effort?

Not to mention the boys?

"I'm sorry Bess and the kids couldn't make it—"

"Never mind. I'm glad *you* did. Mulled wine or something stronger?"

"Something stronger."

"I thought so." Drew led Grady to the kitchen, where he poured them both a stiff scotch. "Merry Christmas, old friend."

"Merry Christmas." Grady tapped his glass against Drew's before taking a long swallow. "That does hit the spot." He glanced down to see Doug nuzzling his other hand.

Crouching, he scratched the dog behind his ears. "Hello, boy. And a merry Christmas to you. How's he been doing?" Grady asked, looking up at Drew.

"Doug's okay. He's stopped waiting by the door all the time, but he seems kind of bewildered. Poor guy. He's too old to cope with change."

"He's not the only one." Grady closed his eyes and took another swallow from his glass.

Oh, God. Drew's heart fell. Something bad was happening here, and he felt powerless to help.

"Hello, Grady." Mallory emerged from the crowd in the living room and kissed Grady's cheek.

It was a friendly kiss, nothing more. Still, Drew had a crazy urge to step between them. But he controlled himself and instead sipped his scotch, though his eyes narrowed when Grady rested his hand on Mallory's shoulder.

"Pregnancy really does suit you," Grady was

saying, and while Drew couldn't have agreed more, he also wished he'd been the one to say it.

"Not for the first three months it didn't," Mallory replied. "Isn't that right, Drew?"

Her smile bathed him in warmth, and he felt his resentment fade. Grady and Mallory were just friends. What was he thinking?

"By the way." Mallory turned back to Grady. "Claire and Kirk said to say hi. You just missed them. They slipped out while Drew was getting Buddy and Patricia their mulled wine. They had to take the girls home to hang their stockings and put out cookies for Santa."

"I remember those days." Grady stared into his drink, a melancholy expression settling over his face.

Mallory shot Drew a distressed look, but her tone was cheerful when she spoke. "What do you mean, remember? Don't tell me you're not going to hang your stocking and set out some goodies, Grady Hogan. I always do."

Grady smiled, although it appeared to take an effort. "And in the morning, is your stocking full?"

"Overflowing." She reached up to give him a hug. "One day yours will be again, too. Maybe sooner than you think."

"I don't know, Mallory. But you're right. Christmas is a time for optimism. One good thing, we've managed to keep Drew in Port Carling for better than two months now. The *Hub of the Lakes Gazette* has never looked better. Forgive me, Angie, for saying so, but it's true.''

Drew hadn't wanted to change the way his mother had done things. Mostly, he'd kept putting out the paper just to keep himself busy while he tried to sort out the future in his mind.

But of course his own personality was leaving its stamp. Not only in the editorials but in more obvious ways. Such as the new column he'd added, ''The Cottage Correspondent,'' where he tried to link world happenings to the day-to-day trivia of life in Port Carling.

It was fun. It kept him amused. But he knew he was just marking time, waiting for something to happen, for some voice out of the sky to tell him what to do.

Sell the paper, sell the house, give Doug to Mallory. That was what he kept waiting to hear, but so far the words weren't coming in clearly enough.

He had a feeling Mallory was standing between him and the speakers. Their friendship had deepened since his mother's death. He'd leaned on his best friend to make it through these past few months, and he couldn't imagine doing without her. At least not yet.

Then there was the pregnancy. Every week brought some change, some new development. Even though his was hardly the involvement of a typical father, he still didn't want to miss anything. He was beginning to think it would make sense for him to wait until the baby was born, then go back to Ottawa.

CHAPTER TEN

"PASS THE SANDWICHES, PLEASE," lisped Lisa, Terese Balfour's three-year-old daughter.

Terese looked embarrassed at her daughter's appetite, but Mallory was glad the little girl was eating her fill. Once the child was finished, Mallory let her play with the box of teddy bears she'd removed from her Christmas tree earlier that day. Terese insisted on helping her do the dishes in the kitchen.

"That was a lovely lunch. Thanks so much for inviting us."

"You're welcome. I'm sorry it took so long to get organized." January had already arrived and Mallory had meant to invite the small family to lunch ages ago. But Christmas had been such a rush, and Terese had turned down an invitation to join them all at Drew's on Christmas Eve.

Mallory was still hoping she and Terese could be friends, but the young mother's reserve was pretty difficult to get around. Mallory's pregnancy at least gave them a safe topic of conversation.

"When are you due?" Terese asked while she washed dishes.

"April 14."

"How are you feeling?"

"Great ever since the nausea passed."

"Not nice, is it? Not to mention the exhaustion."

"I suppose it's even worse after you have the baby and have night feedings and everything. Was Lisa a good baby?"

"Oh, she had a cranky first few months. Her crying really drove my husband nuts...." Two parallel grooves appeared between Terese's brows.

Mallory was reminded of Lisa's comment about her father hitting her. The little girl had said nothing about her dad since then, and neither had Terese.

Mallory had noticed a scar, though. About an inch long, reaching out from the corner of Terese's right eye. It was probably an innocent mark from a childhood accident of some sort.

But now Terese must have caught her looking at it, because she brushed it with her fingers. "My ex wasn't violent at first. Not till after the baby was born. She wasn't planned, and she brought out the very worst in him. I didn't want to believe it, though. I thought he needed time to adjust, that eventually his behavior would improve."

"But it didn't?"

"No. Actually deciding to leave was the hardest. Once that was behind me..." She shrugged. "Have you started your prenatal classes yet?"

"I'm supposed to begin next week." Once a week, for seven weeks, her doctor had told her.

"You should ask a friend to be your birthing partner," the doctor had also said.

That had thrown Mallory into a quandary. She'd wanted to ask Claire—with three girls of her own, she was more than qualified—but didn't feel she could. Claire would have to drive up from Toronto, arrange baby-sitters for her girls. And what if she couldn't make it to Bracebridge in time for the baby's birth? It would be better to ask someone from Port Carling.

Someone like...Drew?

In several ways, the choice was obvious. Drew was her best friend. He was the baby's father.

But in other ways, it wasn't so easy. Drew was having a hard time coming to terms with this pregnancy. It wasn't as real to him as it was to her. Probably because he didn't want this baby the way she did. Would prenatal classes be more reality than he was ready for?

Plus, given the unstable state of their relationship, would it really be wise to request his help with something so intimate? In the old days, sure, she wouldn't have hesitated. But now...simple touches were not so simple anymore.

Nor were simple kisses. Like at his Christmas Eve party, under the mistletoe. His kiss had been sweet; not too long, but not short, either. If she and Drew had been alone, if they hadn't been interrupted, who knew what might have happened....

Yeah, right. They'd gone down that road once before; she doubted Drew would be eager to repeat the mistake.

With Terese washing, and Mallory drying and putting away, the two women did the dishes in no time.

"I have a present for Lisa before you go," Mallory said, pulling a wrapped parcel from under her now-naked tree.

"Oh, but we can't—" Terese raised her hands to her face.

"Please. Let me," Mallory insisted. "I love Christmas—especially buying gifts for children."

Lisa dropped the bears she was playing with. "Is that for me?" She looked from Mallory to her mother. When Terese nodded, Mallory gave her the package. Lisa tore off the paper, then opened the large box to find the red snowsuit they'd first admired in her shop.

"Mallory, that's too much..." Terese protested.

"But it's perfect for her. And I was going to mark it down anyway."

Lisa already had the jacket on. "Do I look pretty?"

"Yes, you do, honey," Terese said. Glancing at Mallory, she added, "And warm. Thank you, Mallory."

"My pleasure."

Mallory went to the front window and watched them leave, mother and daughter, hand in hand. Lisa's red snowsuit stood out against the white landscape for blocks.

She knew her instincts had been right. She and Terese would make good friends. Already she felt a level of comfort with the young mother that she had with only a handful of people.

But an aura of mystery surrounded Terese still. Although she'd told Mallory about her husband and why she'd had to flee from him, there was so much she hadn't confided. And some details about Terese's life in Port Carling didn't make sense.

Such as why she wouldn't give Mallory her phone number when Mallory asked for it.

"FOR GOD'S SAKE, LOOK OUT!"

Mallory heard Drew hollering from behind as she tucked low over her cross-country skis and sailed down the hill, her feet firmly planted in the twin furrows groomed into the crisp, cold snow. Her braided hair flew behind her, and the wind whipped tears into her eyes.

The day was clear and cold and they were nearly at the end of the five-mile circuit they'd started an hour earlier. But Drew was being a pain, insisting she take the hills slower than usual. As the ground leveled in front of her, Mallory glanced over her shoulder. Seconds later Drew was beside her, shaking his head.

"I can't handle it anymore," he said.

"What do you mean?"

"Watching you ski. The way you go down those hills. You could slow down a little, you know."

"And you worry too much. The doctor said I could continue with my normal activities."

"He probably didn't know you like to ski as if terrorists are pursuing you. Have you ever thought what would happen if you fell?"

"When was the last time you saw me lose my balance on an easy course like this?"

"Okay, I give up." With a couple of long strides he was in front of her, making short work of the last hundred yards.

She observed him, enjoying the graceful rhythm of his strokes. He cut a mean figure in his close-fitting Nordic ski outfit, his legs long and lean, his shoulders broad and powerful. When she caught up to him, he was already loading his skis onto the roof rack of her car.

"By the way," she said, huffing slightly from the exertion of following his pace, "I have something to ask you."

"Yeah?" He bent to help her remove her skis, then put them up on the rack for her. "You want some pointers on how to snowplow?"

She leaned against the side of the car. "Very

funny. Actually, I was wondering if you'd be my birthing partner.''

She hadn't meant to just blurt out her request. In the silence that followed, she realized what a mistake she'd made. "Of course, if you'd rather not, I'd understand—"

"Hang on." Drew locked the rack, then gave her his full attention. "I'm sorry if I'm acting a little stunned. It's just—well, what exactly would you want me to do?"

"Help me when the baby comes."

"You mean, in the delivery room?"

She nodded. He'd turned a little pale, and she remembered that he'd always shied away from medical situations. "I could always ask—"

"So I'd be right there when our baby was born?"

"Yes." The way he said "our" chased away the winter cold, warming her right to the tips of her fingers.

"I think I'd like that." Drew dug the toe of his boot into the packed snow, then gave her a sideways look. "Thanks for asking, Mal. I'll try not to faint or anything."

Mallory smiled and climbed into the passenger seat. "Thanks for asking," he'd said. And she was so glad she had.

"BIRTHING PARTNER," Drew muttered. He was only too glad to help Mallory in any way he could, but she'd failed to mention that he'd have to attend seven prenatal classes before the big event.

Now he glanced around the gym floor where he and Mallory, along with several other couples, were gathered in front of a perky community nurse named Stacey. She was in her early forties, an attractive blonde with a lilting voice and lots of energy.

From peace treaties and no-fly zones to boating regulations and prenatal classes. How his life had changed. It would be laughable if it wasn't so damn frightening. In fact things were changing so fast sometimes he didn't know who he was anymore. He'd stare at the bathroom mirror for minutes on end, wondering who on earth was staring back.

Beside him, Mallory was listening raptly to everything Stacey had to say. They'd spent the first fifteen minutes introducing themselves. Five of the six other couples in the room were obviously married; the other was a young girl of about seventeen and her older sister, who was acting as her birthing partner.

Drew felt sorry for the young girl; she obviously felt scared. And out-of-place. Which she was. She should have been painting her fingernails blue—or whatever bizarre colors kids were into these days— and laughing with her friends; not sitting on this cold wooden floor, listening to a talk on nutrition and the growing baby.

He turned to Mallory. Did she ever feel her life

was spinning out of control? She never let on if she did. As far as he could tell, she considered this baby the best thing that had ever happened to her.

Of course, Mallory was a mature woman, with her own home and financial security—a far cry from the little seventeen-year-old's situation.

But still, didn't Mallory get nervous? At least sometimes?

Drew shifted his attention back to the front of the room, where Stacey was now talking about the role the birthing partner could play in making the expectant mother's life more comfortable.

"Some of you probably feel a little guilty when you think of all your partner is going through. But you can help! Massage is one of the techniques that can ease an expectant mother's aches and pains. It also comes in handy during the actual birthing process, but we won't be getting into that until the last couple of weeks."

Drew put his hand over Mallory's. It felt cold and he wondered if she was anxious. Was she regretting having chosen him as her birthing partner? She'd looked so unsure of herself when she'd asked. And her voice had been apologetic, as if she'd expected him to say no.

Afterward, he'd wondered if she'd been *hoping* he'd say no. If maybe she'd asked him out of courtesy, as the baby's father.

I won't let you down, he promised her silently.

He was glad she'd given him this chance to help. And awed that he would be there for his baby's first breath.

"Let's start with the lower back, please," Stacey was saying. "Expectant mothers often experience a lot of pain here. Not only during pregnancy, but delivery, as well. If the women would just lie on their sides like this—" Stacey demonstrated. "Then I'll show your partners some of the massage techniques they can try."

Now Mallory was stretched out on the gym floor, and *he* was expected to massage her. Drew put a hand on the cotton T-shirt that covered her back and tried to follow Stacey's directions.

"Rub your thumbs in circles like this. Apply a little pressure, then move outward."

The technique felt awkward to Drew, and he worried he was being more irritating than helpful. He leaned over to whisper in Mallory's ear.

"You never told me you had backaches."

"I didn't before. But now that I'm on this hard gym floor…"

He grinned and attempted to dig his thumbs in the way the instructor had demonstrated, but for some reason that made Mallory giggle. "Drew, you're tickling me!"

"Are you criticizing my massage technique?" He shifted his hands, then started a soft rubbing in the very small of her back.

Suddenly, he realized that Stacey was standing beside them. "Good try, Drew, but you've got to really get in there. Don't be afraid to touch her." She bent over and directed his hands firmly.

Beginning to catch on, Drew spanned the width of Mallory's back with his hands, pressing his thumbs into the muscles helping to support the weight of the baby.

"Is this better?" he asked, bending low over Mallory's head.

"I'll say."

Her voice purred rather sexily, he thought. Which was an odd observation to have about a pregnant woman during a prenatal class.

But not so odd when you looked at Mallory. She shone. In her case, beauty was so much more than the long line of a slender leg or the pretty curve of a woman's smile. Her mossy eyes sparkled with intelligence, honesty, directness; you could see her kindness and patience in the curve of her lips.

She was such a great person. How did she manage to put up with him? Impulsively, he dropped a kiss on the top of her head. Surprised, she glanced up at him. A question knotted her brow.

"You were so sweet to agree to do this for me. Are you hating it?"

"Not at all." And it was true.

"I feel like such a cow, lying on the floor in my pregnancy duds."

"You don't look like a cow. You look...nice."
Now, there was an inspired description. But what
would she have said if he'd told her she looked
sexy? She'd probably have given him a kick with
those jazzy runners she was wearing.

Yet it was true, Mallory was sexy in her pregnancy; there was no denying it. Her body curved
sensuously under her loose clothing. He couldn't
touch her without being aware of the roundness of
her hips, the swell of her breasts, the fresh herbal
scent of her hair.

Inappropriate thoughts for prenatal class, he was
sure. He tried to concentrate on the small of her
back. Digging in his thumbs, he focused on muscles
and ligaments and knots and pains.

But the small of a woman's back was a pretty
sexy place. And he had a distinct memory of kissing
Mallory there once.

"Drew, that feels really good."

"It does, doesn't it?" He was really getting into
this massage thing. Almost without thinking, he'd
slipped his hands under the cotton of her top. Her
skin was soft and warm, and the curve of her back
just seemed to invite his hands to slide forward onto
the soft mound of her tummy.

Lord, even that felt sexy to him.

"Drew." The word was a breath of sweet air.

He returned his hands to the small of her back
and inched up until he encountered the thick strap

of her maternity bra. Which should have been a major turnoff, but wasn't because it made him think of the heavy, ripe breasts that needed all that support.

"Um, Mallory?"

"Yes?"

"I think I'm enjoying this more than you are. Is that allowed?"

"Drew, stop teasing. We fat pregnant women are sensitive."

But he wasn't teasing. Not at all. "Do you get to massage me, too? Because I know just the place that needs it—"

She pushed at him, laughing. "Behave yourself, Drew."

"But what if I can't?"

HE WAS SERIOUS. No, he couldn't be. Drew Driscoll could not be enjoying massaging a pregnant woman on the floor of a high-school gymnasium.

Mallory stared at the painted red line in front of her and tried to imagine the room full of sweaty adolescents playing basketball. *Take a deep breath,* she told herself. *Imagine Claire is giving you the massage.* After all, this was supposed to be *relaxing* and *enjoyable.*

Oh, it was enjoyable all right. But hardly relaxing. There was no way she could forget, not even for an instant, that *Drew's* hands were gliding over her back. And that one moment when he'd slid his palms forward to cup her tummy...

To have found that arousing was too weird. But she had.

"There are various products available that might help with your massaging technique." Stacey was back at the front of the class, holding a contraption with wooden balls connected by contorted lengths of blue plastic. It looked like a bug.

"Here." She passed it to Drew. "Give this a try. Apply light pressure with your palm and allow it to roll over her."

Mallory laughed as the massager ran a line up the side of her back. "You're tickling me again. Stay in the center."

Drew passed the contraption to the next couple. "I prefer my hands."

So did she. Oh, so did she. Mallory closed her eyes, but that made her thoughts veer dangerously from pregnant women and basketball to Drew with his hands on her body.

All too reminiscent of their magical weekend last July. He'd run his hands over her back then, too. She remembered him rolling her on her tummy and trailing kisses from the base of her neck to the hollow in her back. The very place he was now rubbing in a circular motion...

She opened her eyes and forced herself to look

around the room, to concentrate on the other couples in the class.

The man and woman sitting diagonally from her and Drew had caught her eye when she'd first walked in. They were in their midtwenties, she would guess. The man was blond and athletic; his wife was also fair, and petite. Their wedding rings were so new they sparkled in the fluorescent lighting.

What made the couple stand out, at least to Mallory, was the way they gazed at each other. As if they shared a delightful secret. They'd held hands throughout Stacey's introduction, and occasionally the woman rested her head against the man's shoulder.

The easy intimacy between the two bespoke love and commitment. Mallory especially noticed the glow in the man's eyes when they fell to his pregnant wife's belly. He kept reaching out to pat it, as though to reassure himself, that they really were going to have a baby.

It was sweet. It was romantic.

Why, then, was Mallory wishing she had a basketball in her hands so she could throw it at them?

Because she was jealous. Because she yearned to have someone sitting next to her who looked at her like that. Someone who wanted this baby as much as she did.

Oh, Lord. Mallory swallowed. Drew had withdrawn his hands from under her T-shirt and was now massaging her shoulders and the base of her neck. That was good, because it was safer—since it didn't cloud her mind with dangerous thoughts and dangerous memories.

It wasn't *someone* she wanted. It was Drew and only Drew. Partly because he was her baby's father, but mostly because she loved him.

Over the years she would have been the first to admit she had a crush on Drew; even that she'd set him up as an ideal that few—or none—of the men she dated could ever meet.

But she'd never before admitted any of these feelings were serious. How could she? Drew was wonderful, but he was not big on commitment. Over the years she'd seen lots of women pass through his life, while her friendship with him had stayed constant. Implicitly, she'd understood why. *She* was the best friend. *They* were the lovers.

She'd always accepted that. Why not now? Was it because they'd made love that weekend? Was it the baby? Or was it simply having him back in her life, living next door in Port Carling, seeing him every day?

Who knew? And what did it matter? Knowing why wouldn't change the fact that she'd fallen in love with her best friend and could no longer pretend it wasn't so.

She wasn't a teenager with a crush anymore. She

was thirty-five years old and pregnant. Too old for crushes, and too wise for self-deception.

She loved Drew. It was so obvious. Why had she needed to be hit over the back with a wooden massager to see it?

"HOW'S BUSINESS?"

Mallory had purposefully turned her back to the door when she'd recognized Drew through the panes of glass. Now she glanced over her shoulder.

"Not bad. Of course, when almost everything in the store is marked down forty percent..." It was almost like giving the merchandise away. Still, she needed to clear out the old winter stock. Despite the fact that Port Carling was socked in with snow, that there were still months of winter left to contend with, it was time for retailers to start planning for spring.

"I rented that video you've been eager to catch. The one with Julia Roberts." Drew lifted the plastic case in the air for her to see.

"Oh." Well, so much for begging off from their usual Friday pizza and video. She'd been planning to tell him she was tired, which wasn't really true. The truth was she was afraid of spending time with him, afraid he might realize how she really felt....

"You don't sound all that excited." Snowflakes dusted the shoulders of Drew's leather coat and his dark hair. As she watched, the flakes melted into little drops of water.

"It's been a busy week." She refolded a sweater that a potential customer had left in a mess, then she stopped to straighten a blouse on a hanger.

"Can I help?"

"No, that's okay. I'm just about finished." She reached for the night deposit and reviewed it to make sure everything was in order. After a moment she glanced up, aware that Drew was studying her.

He was a journalist. Trained to notice things. Had he guessed already that she was in love with him? "Maybe we should cancel tonight, Drew. I don't feel I'll be good company."

"I'll be in charge of the scintillating conversation," he assured her cheerfully. "All you have to do is sit back and relax."

"Scintillating? That'll be a first."

Relief showed in his smile. He stepped forward to tug on her ponytail. "I'll even order your favorite pizza. See?" he said as she went to the back room for her coat and purse. "There's nothing I won't do to please you tonight."

"Really?" Now, there was a loaded offer.

"Pickles. Ice cream. You name it."

"Oh, Drew…" Logic told her she should keep her distance. If her best friend had any idea what she really wanted, he'd backpedal on his offer so fast her head would spin.

"Come on." He was smirking. Holding the door for her. How could she resist?

"Okay."

This time. But she was going to have to start seeing less of him. She really was.

THE NEXT MORNING, Drew knew he'd been putting it off long enough. Mallory couldn't help him; Saturday was her busiest day in the shop—especially with the huge sale she was having.

Going through his mother's personal effects was something he'd have to do on his own. He pushed open the door, kicked in two large cardboard boxes and carried in a dark-green plastic garbage bag.

He intended to give away most of her clothes. Some, like her "gardening togs," as she'd called them, would only be fit for the trash. She'd never owned much in the way of jewelry, so that part would be easy to deal with.

What else would he find? He could only guess; he could only hope....

Uppermost in his mind were questions about his father. If Angie had held anything back about the man who'd conceived him, this room was the one place he might find it.

Drew pulled open the curtains, releasing a cloud of dust motes. They hovered in the bright light from the noon sun, and he watched as they defied gravity and hung suspended in the steady flow of air that wafted from the heat register on the floor.

Suspended.

That was how he felt. It had been four months since Angie's death, and he hadn't made a single important decision required of him. His life in Ottawa was still in limbo, while here in Port Carling he was just going through the motions. Not that he wasn't enjoying those motions, but his life had taken on a surreal quality—as if he'd stepped outside his body and was observing it to see how well it did on its own.

Maybe going through Angie's things was step one on the route back to reality. He looked away from the dust motes and surveyed the room. It hadn't changed in twenty years. There was Angie's bedspread—you could hardly see the flowers anymore; they'd all faded out to a bland peach color. A plain wooden chair stood off to one corner, by a small rug that Mallory must have made for her. Opposite the bed was an oval mirror and long dresser that had belonged to his grandmother, and on the one remaining wall, next to the closet, was the higher chest that had been his grandfather's.

The closet was tiny by modern standards. Drew pulled out the few dresses Angie had owned, including the velvet skirt she had worn every Christmas Eve. There were a few blouses, a blazer or two, and that was it. On the top shelf he found a couple of hats and old purses. Down below were her shoes.

He emptied the tall chest next. The top drawer held underwear. Mostly in serviceable beige cotton, except for one racy black silk set.

Way to go, Angie! Drew grinned and went to the next drawer. He made his way through socks and sweat suits, jeans and sweaters. Finishing with the tall chest, he moved to the long dresser, and soon had both boxes filled with clothing for the thrift shop.

It wasn't until he reached the top right-hand drawer that he found anything personal. Here were letters from Angie's friends in Toronto, and the postcards he'd sent from various parts of the world. She'd saved every Mother's Day card he'd ever given her, including one he'd made in kindergarten with a picture of a blue snake on the cover.

A scrapbook held clippings of his articles from the *Globe*. He flipped through the pages, and the old columns reminded him of the adrenaline jolt he always got when he was working on a hot story. Imagine Angie saving all this…

And there were photographs, attached to the stiff, off-white pages with old-fashioned black corners. He laughed at Mallory and him in the tub with their underwear on, and was silent at the sight of him sleeping on his grandpa's lap in the recliner that still sat in the corner of the living room.

At the very bottom of the drawer lay a thin packet of letters, bound with a faded red elastic. They were addressed to the residence Angie had stayed at when she was in journalism at Ryerson in Toronto, and the masculine-looking handwriting was not his grandfather's.

Whose, then? A male admirer's? The letters had to have meant something to Angie or she wouldn't have kept them. Maybe they were from the man she'd left behind in Port Carling. Or perhaps, if Drew was really lucky, they were from his father.

CHAPTER ELEVEN

DREW WAS ALMOST AFRAID to look at the letters he'd found in his mother's top dresser drawer. Bracing himself, he picked up the packet, pulled off the elastic and counted five envelopes, all addressed in that same handwriting. When he turned them over, he saw the same return address written on the back flap.

Buddy Conroy.

Well, well, well. Drew considered the possibilities. Angie could have saved the letters because they were cherished correspondence from an old friend.

Or, Buddy was the hometown sweetheart Angie had left behind to go to college.

His intuition favored the latter.

Only one way to tell. Carefully he lifted the flap on the first envelope and pulled out a folded sheet of legal-size paper.

The salutation said it all.

"My darling, stubborn Angie..."

The next few lines had Drew's cheeks growing hot. Embarrassed, amused, he refolded the pages and stuffed them back inside.

Buddy and his mother. Drew rolled the idea around in his mind a few minutes, then decided he wasn't surprised. Buddy and Angie had been good friends. It was easy to see how they might once have been in love.

But Buddy wasn't Drew's father. His relationship with Drew's mother had ended when Angie left to go to school in Toronto, several years before Drew's conception.

Drew wondered if his mother had ever regretted her decision to break off with Buddy. Or if Buddy had regretted not waiting longer, in case Angie changed her mind. He'd married Patricia by the time Angie returned to Port Carling. Drew remembered Buddy teasing Angie about how she'd been too busy studying to come to the wedding.

But would he have married Patricia if he'd known Angie would be returning, thanks to Angie's pregnancy and her father's stroke?

Drew leaned back in the chair, thinking how capricious fate could be. What would his life have been like if Angie had married Buddy? Of course, Buddy might have backed away from raising another man's son.

Drew collected the letters and slipped the elastic over them again. He was tempted to read them through but felt that would be an invasion of privacy. Buddy, no doubt, wouldn't like it. As for Angie, he had no idea. Maybe she had expected him to find these letters.

Had she left her legal affairs in order, he might have convinced himself of that.

But death had come swiftly, catching her off guard. For all he knew, she would have destroyed the letters, given the chance.

Should he? Surely there was no need for him to hang on to them, especially since he wasn't planning on reading them. After a brief hesitation, Drew tossed the letters into his briefcase. Maybe he should talk to Buddy before he trashed them.

He headed into the kitchen to make coffee. Decaf coffee, on the off chance he could talk Mallory into joining him for a cup when she got home from the store.

Some afternoon. He rubbed the back of his neck, disappointed that he hadn't found any of the answers he'd been searching for.

Did it matter? Drew poured boiling water into the French press and thought about his childhood. He'd been happy growing up. He and Angie had always been close, and he'd had a good relationship with his grandpa.

He hadn't needed a father as a youngster. Why on earth did he need one now that he was a grown man?

From the window above the kitchen table, he saw

Mallory step out of her garage. He didn't have to check the clock to know it was shortly after six.

He thought about the baby growing inside her, and wondered what kind of a father he was going to make. A long-distance one, at any rate, which was hardly ideal. And what if Mallory married, eventually? What would his role be then?

Trying to shut off those thoughts, he opened the back door and called out to her.

"Feel like a coffee? I have decaf, or I could make herbal tea." Man, but he was stooping low these days.

She hesitated for a moment, then shook her head. "I don't have time. Claire's coming in from the city and we're having dinner at the Teahouse."

"Okay." That sounded good to him. He waited, expecting her to extend an invitation, but she didn't. She just waved a mittened hand and carried on along the walk he'd shoveled that morning, toward her back door.

Drew closed the door and took a packaged dinner from the freezer. Perhaps Mallory was avoiding him. Ever since that damn prenatal class on Tuesday, she'd acted strange. She'd even tried to cancel out of their pizza and movie last night. He suspected she might have succeeded if he hadn't finessed her by renting that romantic comedy she'd wanted to see.

Now he thought back to the conversation they'd

had—or rather, hadn't had, after the movie was over. It had been early, just past ten. Usually, they chatted until almost midnight. Last night, she'd practically thrown him out the door.

"Tired?" he'd asked, when she'd pressed the eject button, then handed him the rewound tape.

"Sort of."

Liar. She hadn't yawned once the entire movie. So why the big hurry to get him out of there? He felt she owed him some answers before he left.

"Is something wrong?"

"Of course not."

Now, there was a dead giveaway. In his experience, whenever a woman said nothing was wrong, something always was. And it usually had to do with commitment.

When she'd first told him she was pregnant, she'd been so full of assurances that she would have the baby on her own, that she wouldn't expect anything from him and that their friendship wouldn't change.

Maybe she'd believed it at the time.

But he was willing to bet she didn't feel it anymore.

How did she feel? Did she want him to marry her?

On the surface, that wasn't a bad idea. He had to admit it had occurred to him. They were definitely compatible. Being the best of friends had to be a strong foundation for marriage. And he found her attractive. More and more each day, it seemed.

So why not get married and give this baby a father?

A real play-catch-every-night and tuck-you-into-bed father. The kind who was there when you went to sleep and there when you woke in the morning.

The kind he hadn't had.

Drew thought again of the man he'd never known and probably never would. He'd grown up just fine without him, he told himself again. Angie had done a great job, and it was clear Mallory was planning on following in her footsteps.

That marriage idea—it was all in his head, not in hers.

Now, standing in his kitchen, drinking the decaf coffee by himself, he wondered if maybe that was why she'd been giving him the cold shoulder lately. Maybe she was trying to let him know she didn't need his help as much as he felt she did.

Drew knew he should feel relieved that she was so independent. Then why wasn't he?

"How was dinner with Claire?" he asked Mallory the next morning. They were in his mother's Explorer, cross-country skis on the roof rack and travel mugs of coffee in the cup holders on the dash. They'd just left Port Carling, headed for the cross-country ski trails in Port Sydney, less than an hour away.

"Okay."

Mallory took a sip of her coffee and he waited for her to comment on it. He'd brewed the decaf especially for her, but she said nothing.

"So how was dinner at the Teahouse?" He was still miffed she hadn't asked him along. He'd ended up spending the night by himself, watching television. He'd phoned the Hogans', to see if Warren and Taylor felt like going to a movie, but they were out with their friends. And Grady and Bess had plans with friends, too.

"People from Barrie," Grady had grumbled. Bess had just taken a job with an insurance firm in the town, which was on the highway between Port Carling and Toronto.

"She'll spend half her time driving and half her money buying gas" was Grady's contention. Obviously, he wasn't thrilled with his wife's decision.

"It was okay," Mallory said in answer to Drew's question.

"And Claire?"

"She was okay, too."

"Not feeling too chatty this morning, are you?"

He'd expected her to give him her old smile and apologize for her strange mood. Instead, she sank into her seat.

"I've got a lot on my mind, okay? I told you I wasn't sure if I was up to skiing today."

A few minutes passed in silence. And they weren't comfortable ones. He didn't think it was skiing she wasn't up to. It was spending time with him. But what had he done? Had his massage technique been that bad? Drew eased up on the accelerator and reached over to squeeze her leg.

"If you've got a lot on your mind, then why won't you talk to me about it? For a week all you've been saying is that nothing's wrong, when something obviously is. Don't try to deny it."

He put his hand back on the wheel and shot another glance at her. She still wouldn't look at him, damn it. This was starting to frighten him. "Is everything okay with the baby? You had a doctor's appointment on Thursday, didn't you?"

Mallory's face was pale. "Yes, I did, and everything's fine. The baby's growing. Her heart rate is healthy...."

"So?"

"Oh, Drew." She ran a hand along the tight black leggings she wore for skiing. "Maybe I did the wrong thing asking you to be my birthing partner. What if you have to go back to Ottawa before the baby is born?"

Relief had him easing back in his seat. "Is that all? Hell, Mal, you don't have to worry. I wouldn't have said I'd do it if I hadn't planned to be here."

Mallory didn't reply, so he continued. "And I've been thinking about staying for a while after the birth, too. Just to make sure you're settled."

Mallory's prolonged silence made him wonder if he hadn't understood properly. Perhaps Mallory was sorry she'd asked him to be her birthing partner because what she really wanted was for him to *leave*.

"I plan on being part of this baby's life, Mal. I've thought about what you said, and being a family friend or some kind of fake uncle just isn't going to cut it for me. I know it'll be hard with me living in Ottawa, but having a part-time father is better than no father at all. Isn't it?"

"That's great, Drew. I'm really glad."

Until that moment he hadn't realized how desperately he'd wanted her to approve of his decision. Her words were positive, yet he was disappointed she didn't sound more enthusiastic. Didn't she want him involved with this baby? He was about to ask her that when his scanner suddenly came to life.

He recognized the voice of Constable Cooper, from the local RCMP detachment.

"Sounds like kids have gotten into another cottage," Cooper was saying to the dispatcher. "Can you give me directions? I'm just leaving Bracebridge now."

Drew listened as the dispatcher explained where the trouble was. He glanced at Mallory.

"We're about fifteen minutes ahead of Cooper. Mind if I turn back and check things out?"

"Go for it." She gripped the dash as he pulled into a drive and swung around in the direction they'd just come from.

The cottage was a ten minute drive away on the east side of Lake Rosseau, only a stone's throw from the Ridgeways' vacation home. Smoke was drifting from the chimney when they arrived, and a rusted Datsun sat in the drive.

"Looks like the kind of car kids would use," Drew commented. "They've been here for a while. The tracks are snowed in already." He parked out on the road so Constable Cooper would be able to draw the same conclusion, then stepped out of the Explorer into a foot of soft powder.

"Do you know who owns this place?" he asked Mallory.

She nodded. "The MacDougals are a retired couple. They spend their winters in Florida."

"Perfect setup for vandals." He scanned the white carpet of snow, seeing nothing except a few scratches from birds and the distinctive markings from a rabbit or two. "Stay here. I'll go check the windows."

"Like heck I'll stay here," Mallory muttered, following in his tracks.

With a sigh of resignation he paused, waiting for her to catch up. Then, taking her arm, he walked around to the back of the house, where, predictably, he found large picture windows overlooking the view of the lake. Crouching, he blocked the light with his arm and took a quick look inside.

"Somebody's in there, all right." Relief made his shoulder muscles loosen. It wasn't Taylor or Warren or any other teenagers, as he'd feared. "Looks like a woman and a child. They're sitting by the fire, reading. Maybe the MacDougals gave their keys to their kids."

"They don't have any children," Mallory said. She moved in front of him, and he held her waist as she leaned forward to see for herself.

"Oh, no!" She pulled back from the window.

"What's wrong? Do you know them?"

"I sure do. Drew, it's Terese. The single mother I told you about. And her daughter, Lisa."

"THANK YOU FOR TALKING the constable out of pressing charges," Terese said hours later in Mallory's kitchen. Mallory had a container of frozen chili thawing in the microwave and was busy slathering butter on a loaf of French bread to make garlic toast.

"Hey. No problem." Drew was slouched over the kitchen table, resting his chin in the palm of his hand. His expression as he watched Terese was a combination of sympathy and concern, and for some reason Mallory had a choked-up feeling just looking at him. She blinked and focused back on Terese.

"I'm sure the MacDougals will understand when I explain." She'd already called their Florida number and left a message for them to phone her.

"It was a stupid thing to do." Terese pushed a hand through her short dark hair. Her brown eyes looked enormous and shone with unshed tears.

"You were obviously desperate," Drew said.

Mallory felt horribly guilty. She'd known Terese was low on money, but it had never occurred to her to wonder if she and her daughter had a place to live. Mallory had never known someone who was homeless. What a shock to realize that homelessness could happen to ordinary people—even families with children.

"Yes, well…" Terese glanced at Lisa, who was coloring a rainbow she'd drawn. "We left our house on the spur of the moment. All I took with me was one suitcase and my car. I stopped at the bank to clean out the checking account, but there wasn't much money in it. I've been hoping to get a job. With a small child, though, it's been hard."

Mallory didn't imagine there were many openings in Port Carling in January. Maybe by the time spring rolled around…

"You'll stay with me until you find something."

Terese looked startled. "That's a kind offer. But I can't accept—"

"Where else are you going to go?"

Terese had no answer to that.

"I have an extra room. It won't be any trouble."

"A three-year-old in your house won't be any trouble?" Terese eyed her skeptically. "No way, Mallory. It's just too much."

"You wouldn't say that if you knew Mallory," Drew interjected.

"Besides," Mallory added, "I can use the experience." She smoothed her fleece sweatshirt over her rounded belly.

"It won't be for long," Drew added. "Something tells me you're going to settle into Port Carling easier than you think. When's dinner, Mal?"

"About half an hour."

"Why don't I take the squirt over to my house for a while to play on the computer. Ever heard of *The Magic School Bus?*" he asked Lisa.

The little girl shook her head solemnly.

"Lisa doesn't watch much TV."

"That's okay." He turned to the child. "You're going to love it. Coming?"

Lisa set down her crayon and checked her mother's face. Seeing approval, she slid off her chair. "Okay, mister. Take me to the bus." She held out her hand.

Drew retrieved her red snow jacket and helped her on with the garment. "It isn't a real bus..." he was explaining as they went out the door.

Mallory pulled lettuce, celery and tomatoes from the fridge. After setting them on the counter, she noticed Terese staring at the closed door with an expression that was almost dreamy.

"What a nice man."

Mallory swallowed, then selected her sharpest knife. "Yes."

"And so good-looking. I've never seen eyes like that before. Such a vivid shade of blue. Almost like this crayon." Terese drew a line across a clean sheet of paper, then picked up the crayon to read the label. "'Midnight-blue.'"

Mallory rinsed the celery and started chopping. Drew was good-looking, all right, and it was the rare woman who didn't notice.

"Are you and he...?" Terese had risen to wash her hands; now she was tearing the lettuce.

Mallory focused on chopping the celery. "No."

"Okay. I'm sorry if I'm prying. There did seem to be something between you."

Mallory brushed back a wisp of hair. "We've been friends forever. We grew up in these houses, lived next door to each other until Drew left Port Carling to go to college."

"That sounds nice. We moved a lot when I was growing up. I would have liked to have a friend like that."

"It *is* nice." Or it had been. Until she'd been fool enough to fall in love with him. Why had she been so stupid? She was the original homebody, whereas Drew had been born with wanderlust in his veins. She didn't doubt that he cared for her—in fact, that he'd do almost anything to make her happy.

But settle in Port Carling? Never.

She could just imagine the panic in his eyes if she'd dared to say that what she really wanted was for him to stay in Port Carling after the baby was born. Stay forever.

CHAPTER TWELVE

MONDAY. DREW SAT AT HIS DESK, gathering his thoughts for the weekly editorial.

"I'm off to have lunch with the mayor." Barry, his full-time reporter, paused at the front door.

"Tell her hello from me," Drew said without looking up. "Ask her when city council's going to approve funds for a homeless shelter."

It was a joke, but after the events of yesterday, it was a poor one.

Drew had felt stricken to realize that Terese and her daughter, Lisa, had no place to live, that they'd actually been moving from one vacant cottage to another for about four months now.

What a darn shame that someone could be in desperate need of shelter while all those fancy places people had the nerve to call cottages went empty. He didn't blame Terese for what she'd done, even though it was illegal.

Thank heavens Mallory had given her another option.

He looked out the window. Across the street was Steamboat Bay and Mallory's store. She was there now, doing her year-end inventory. She wanted to get the accounting organized and her tax returns filed well in advance of the baby's birth.

He'd helped her a little this morning before coming in to write his editorial. He hoped she didn't overdo it this afternoon. She kept saying she was feeling fine and he shouldn't worry, but she *was* pregnant. It seemed to him she ought to be cutting back on her activities even if her doctor said there was no cause.

A gust of wind set the windowpanes rattling. The forecast called for more snow—just what they didn't need. The eighty-year-old building strained under the weight of the snow that had already fallen.

Thank heavens he didn't have to worry about ancient press equipment. Angie had definitely kept up with the times. All the copy was written on, and laid out by, computer now. On press day, which was Tuesday, the computer-generated copy was taped to flats, then taken to the back room for printing. Finished papers were delivered to the post office so subscribers could receive the weekly issue on Wednesday.

Drew knew each step of the process by heart. He'd grown up on the smell of ink and paper, and the *clack, clack* of the presses as they churned out copies was as soothing to him as a lullaby. Angie had loved to tell how she'd only had to take her fussing baby to the office on press day to have him fall instantly asleep.

Drew peered at the blank computer screen in front of him. Before he knew it, his fingers were moving and words appeared: Only In The Big City?

He hit Enter two times, then switched from centered to left-justified alignment. Pausing, he gazed around the room.

Barry's chair was empty, his computer monitor dark. Against the far wall Drew could see the backs of the two women who worked on the classified section. Counting the two men in the print room, the *Gazette* employed six people full-time. Whatever decision he made about staying or leaving would affect them all.

Would affect the whole town.

A newspaper unified a community the way few other things could. It facilitated communication, the dissemination of information, the airing of views. Not many people understood that the way Drew did—his grandfather, then his mother had drilled the importance of journalism into him from an early age.

Drew sighed.

Then returned his gaze to the computer. There was a whole lot of white space under that headline. Time he started typing.

A FEW HOURS LATER, Drew had his editorial. He was tired and ready to go home, but he had to do something first. Once in the Explorer, he drove to the Hogans'.

He only had to get out of the vehicle to know the twins were home from school. A Honda Civic Hatchback sat parked in the driveway and Drew rang the doorbell.

Taylor peeked out from the front window. A few seconds later, the throbbing of the bass stopped and the door opened. As Drew stepped inside, the first thing he noticed was the smell of tobacco smoke.

After glancing around at the four teenagers gathered in the Hogan living room, he decided that he should be glad cigarette smoke was all it was.

In addition to Taylor and Warren, a tall, scrawny boy with acne scars on his cheeks and a ring through his bottom lip was present. Sitting beside him was a girl, her hair bleached white and her skin sickly pale.

"What's up, Drew?" Taylor asked. He had one hand on the door frame, the other stuffed in his baggy jeans. He'd uttered the words casually, but his eyes kept shifting to his brother, who sat on the sofa, arms crossed rebelliously over his chest.

"Checking up on us, I'd guess," Warren said.

Drew shook his head. "No. I came to apologize."

"Yeah?" Warren looked suspicious.

Drew stepped farther inside. "Better shut the door, Taylor, or you'll have a snowbank in the front hall.'' The promised snow was falling in handfuls. He had to make this trip quick so he'd be home in time to shovel the walks before Mallory got in from work.

He removed his boots, then sat across from Warren. After a few seconds, Taylor joined his brother.

"You guys alone here?"

Warren shrugged. "Dad's at the shop. Mom's working. Yeah, we're alone. What's it to you?"

"Nothing. I guess. Just curious." He couldn't see any ashtrays or cigarette packs. The twins must have cleaned up before opening the door. He wondered if the smell of smoke would be gone by the time their parents arrived home, and doubted it.

"About a month ago I insinuated you two might have had something to do with vandalizing some local cottages. I found out yesterday that I was wrong. The details will be in Wednesday's paper, but I wanted to come here to apologize to you guys."

Maybe he should have just saved his breath. The twins were looking at him as if he were standing on the other side of a glass wall and they couldn't hear a word he was saying.

Drew cast his mind back. Fifteen. How had it felt? The big fight for independence—that was what it had all been about. But there had been some fear, too. No matter how tough Warren and Taylor were acting, they still needed reassurance from the adults in their lives.

"I also came to offer you a job," Drew added.

Warren's eyebrows went up. Taylor cocked his head.

"Not more snow shoveling," Warren said, skeptical. "We've already got enough. Besides our house, we do Mrs. Jenkins down the street and—"

"No, not shoveling. I was thinking in terms of the paper. And not delivering it, either. I wondered if you'd like to be part-time sports reporters."

Well, that brightened their eyes, at least. Now they looked as though they were really listening.

"I thought you could attend the local hockey games in the winter, ball games in the summer, and do little write-ups for me. Maybe get a few pictures. You guys know how to use a camera?"

They exchanged glances. "The basics," Warren said slowly.

"Barry could share some pointers. We use a fifty-millimeter lens and a scanner. Gives us pretty good resolution. So what do you say? You up for it?"

"How much time's this going to take?" Warren asked.

Drew squared his shoulders. "Maybe quite a bit."

"We'll do it," Taylor said quickly.

Uncharacteristically, his brother didn't argue. "Yeah. Count us in."

WEDNESDAY MORNING, a little over four thousand copies of the *Hub of the Lakes Gazette* were being perused by subscribers, most from the Port Carling area, others in more distant locations.

In Toronto, Claire had just dropped Jenna off at nursery school before stopping for a latte at a neighborhood coffee shop. She had her copy of the *Gazette* with her, and looked through the paper while she sipped at her hot drink.

Under the headline she read Drew's editorial:

I'm willing to bet most people in Port Carling think homelessness is a big-city problem. That's what I thought, too, until this past Sunday.

"Well, I'll be..." she muttered. "Drew's really making something of the local newspaper. Very interesting...."

MALLORY PLUCKED HER COPY of the *Gazette* out of the mailbox on her way to work and read Drew's editorial while she leaned against the counter, waiting for her first customer:

Around one-thirty in the afternoon on Sunday, Constable Cooper checked out a complaint that smoke was coming from the MacDougals' cottage. Now, everyone knows the MacDougals winter in Florida, so that didn't make sense.

Mallory laughed softly. *"Everyone knows."* He hadn't until she'd told him.

Upon investigation, the constable found a young mother and her three-year-old child had taken up residence in the vacant cottage. The woman had recently left an abusive relationship and was down to her last few dollars.

Poor Terese. Even now, reading about it, Mallory felt awful.

ACROSS TOWN, PATRICIA CONROY WAS drinking coffee and eating banana bread while her husband read the editorial out loud.

"Only three years old!" Patricia shook her head. "Poor baby."

Buddy continued:

"'The young mother was trying to start a new life for her daughter, a wholesome way of life, away from the city. She really likes Port Carling so far, if only she could afford to live here.'"

Buddy set down the paper and looked at his wife. "What do you say to that?"

IT WAS CLOSING TIME, and Drew was alone when Buddy Conroy popped in for a chat.

"Good editorial, Drew. Your mother would have been proud."

"You think so?"

"I know so. It got us thinking, Patricia and me. We have a basement apartment, with a separate entrance out the back. Would that young woman be happy living there?"

"I'm sure she'd be thrilled. But she doesn't have much money."

"That's okay. We wouldn't charge her anything until she gets a job. Even then it would be minimal. Just enough to cover the utilities, maybe a portion of the city taxes, too."

"Buddy, that's fantastic. I can't believe this place. You have no idea how many calls we fielded today. We've got three different job interviews lined up, plus leads on several day cares that charge reasonable baby-sitting fees."

Drew had them all noted on a piece of paper, and now he added Buddy's offer, then put the folded paper in his pocket. He would run over to Mallory's later and give the list to Terese himself.

It made for a good excuse to see Mallory; maybe she'd invite him to stay for dinner. Since the Balfours had moved in, he'd hardly seen her. Except for last night's prenatal class. But she'd been preoccupied then; he supposed that with the baby's arrival drawing closer, that was to be expected.

"Kind of makes you feel good, doesn't it?" Buddy asked.

"Sure does." Drew pulled out a chair on wheels and motioned toward Buddy. "Now that you're here, do you have a few minutes to talk about a private matter?"

Was it his imagination, or did Buddy suddenly look nervous? Nevertheless, the lawyer unbuttoned his parka and sat down willingly.

"I was clearing out Angie's things and I found some letters...."

Man, his desk was a mess. Drew tossed some pens back in the drawer and straightened a stack of paper that had started to topple.

"Anyway..." He took a deep breath and finally managed a glance at Buddy's face. But Buddy wasn't watching him; his attention was caught by something on the wall. Drew didn't have to look to know it was the picture of Angie and her father the day Angie had officially taken over as publisher and editor of the paper.

That had been three months after his grandpa's first stroke and Angie had been obviously pregnant by that time.

"The letters were from you, Buddy. To tell you the truth, I was kind of disappointed. I was hoping to find something from my father."

"Your father?" Buddy's eyes were all lawyer as he shifted his focus from the photograph to the man sitting opposite him. "Don't you waste your time thinking about that man, Drew. You've grown up just fine. Angie did a good job with you on her own."

"I don't say she didn't." But couldn't a man be curious? To want to know the truth about his past, the kind of people he'd come from?

"Back to the letters," he went on. "I have them with me. I was going to drop by your office and give them to you." He pulled the packet out from the side pocket of his briefcase and gave it to the older man.

Buddy's hand, big and strong with wrinkled skin and age spots, trembled just a little as he accepted the letters. He held them up for a moment, then slid off the elastic so he could see them individually.

"Angie and I dated from the time she was sixteen until she left to go to Ryerson," he said. "Your mother ever tell you that?"

"No. But Grandpa used to hint about some man in her past."

"That was me." Buddy smiled, but with a touch of sadness. "I was brokenhearted when she told me she wasn't planning on coming back. She was determined to be a world-class journalist and travel the globe. Just as you've done," he added pointedly.

Drew stared at his own hands, which gripped the

sides of his chair, and wondered. Angie had given up everything for him and for her father. And all he himself had ever done in return was take. She'd always seemed proud of his career. But had she ever wished that one day he'd settle in Port Carling?

"I sent her these letters," Buddy was saying now, "trying to convince her to come back to me. But she never replied. Finally, I gave up. Met Patricia, and it didn't matter so much. But I never stopped caring for your mother. She was always a special friend to me, and to Patricia, too."

Drew nodded. Buddy and Patricia Conroy had always been part of his life. Hell, wasn't it Buddy who'd taught him to fish? Taught him to ride his first two-wheeler, as well.

"Thirty-five years Patricia and I have been married, this June. I figure a man who's been happily wed for that long shouldn't hang on to love letters from another woman." He tossed the packet back on the desk.

Drew didn't know why he felt so surprised. "What should I do with them?"

"Burn them, maybe. It doesn't really matter. Angie was a close friend, and I miss her like crazy, but clinging to the past is a poor way to live a life. You remember that, Drew, when you start thinking of that father of yours again."

"YOU'RE LISTENING to *Foreign Matters,* broadcast every Thursday at eight o'clock...."

Mallory sat down by the radio with her cup of apple-cinnamon tea. Terese was in the back room, putting Lisa to sleep. This would be their last night here. Drew had dropped by yesterday to let them know that the Conroys had a basement apartment available immediately. Today Terese had gone on three job interviews, one with the principal of Brace-bridge High School.

Things were quickly falling into place for the young family, but Mallory wished they could have stayed a little longer. She really got a kick out of Lisa, who always said exactly what was on her mind. And Terese was such a thoughtful houseguest it was a pleasure to have her.

"I'm Drew Driscoll." The warm, husky voice Mallory knew so well swelled up from the radio, filling the small kitchen. "Tonight we're discussing competition in the agriculture industry. Last week in Brussels, European Union farm ministers met to discuss ideas for reforming the common agriculture policy. Here in Canada, we have a new bill being proposed by—"

Mallory remembered the way Drew had hung around last night after passing on the information about the Conroys' apartment. As if waiting for an invitation to dinner.

Had he noticed she was trying to see less of him? Probably. But could he have guessed the reason?

Mallory covered her face with her hands. Just the

possibility of Drew suspecting her true feelings was mortifying. She could imagine the look of pity that would settle over his features. It would end their friendship, she was certain.

If he knew.

"With me today is the federal minister of Agriculture—"

But he couldn't know, or he wouldn't be hanging around so much. Helping her with the store inventory, shoveling her walks, stopping by after work and early in the morning before work. Not to mention spending every Tuesday evening with her at prenatal classes.

As much as Mallory adored Drew, even she admitted he had faults. For one, he usually tended to be a bit self-absorbed. But since he'd found out she was pregnant, he couldn't have been more attentive. Plus, he'd insisted on providing financial support and being part of the baby's life.

It was all much more than she'd expected. And yet...

"What do you say to those critics who claim your government has failed to create a rational, well-thought-out policy on agriculture in this country?"

Trust Drew to go for the jugular. Mallory had listened to enough of his interviews to know that they had a certain rhythm. Generally, he started out with the tough questions, eased up for the middle of the interview, just until his guest had begun to relax, then powered back to the big issues.

Almost like a piece of music. And orchestrated just as carefully. Mallory knew he put in hours of research before each show, and he always took in detailed notes with him.

If only personal lives could be so meticulously managed.

"HOW'S THE INVENTORY GOING?"

Drew's voice startled Mallory, causing her to drop the stack of computer printouts she'd been trying to summarize. Gracefully, he bent over and swooped them up, while she was still catching her breath.

It was Friday, lunchtime, and she'd planned on grabbing a bagel and a glass of milk at Marg's. Now she could feel her cheeks redden and her hands start to tremble.

It's only Drew, she reminded herself. But that didn't reassure her. She couldn't think of him the same old way anymore. She was just so aware of him, all the time now. Today his vitality, the wattage in his smile overwhelmed her cozy, intimate shop.

"Pregnancy must have you off balance. I've never seen you so clumsy." He passed her the papers with a teasing grin.

She was off balance, all right, and pregnancy had nothing to do with it.

"It was quiet in here. You shouldn't have sneaked

up on me.'' Mallory stuffed the inventory sheets into a drawer, then brushed paper dust from her hands.

He appeared skeptical. "There is the bell. I *did* come in the front door.''

Her thoughts had been so wrapped up in him that she hadn't noticed when he'd actually appeared.

"I guess I was preoccupied. I was wondering how Terese and Lisa were settling in over at the Conroys'.'' That was an out-and-out lie, but he'd never know.

"They moved in today?'' He leaned against the counter, stretching out his jean-clad legs and crossing them at the ankle.

He was wearing a black turtleneck with his jeans and a dark-blue down vest that brought out the color of his eyes. He looked so handsome, so overpoweringly male amid the feminine surroundings that her heart ached.

"Yeah. Buddy picked them up this morning. Not that they had much to transport in the way of luggage.''

"At least the Conroys' place comes furnished.''

She nodded. "I'm so proud of you, Drew. That editorial you wrote has made such a difference.''

Drew's smile broadened. "It does seem to have helped, doesn't it? On the drive home from Toronto I thought about all the articles I wrote while working for the *Globe* and even later, when I was freelancing. Lots were pretty good. Some even made people crtically examine things that were happening at the time.''

"Yes, I know." She'd shared some of those successes with him during late-night, long-distance phone calls.

"But I don't think I've ever had such a clear sense of having righted a wrong. It's a small thing. Just one woman and her child. But it feels good. It feels damn good.''

"I'm glad." In the old days she might have touched him. Squeezed his shoulder or given him a hug. Now she was much too conscious of the span of his shoulders, the strength of his arms, of her ever-present desire to have him hold her the way a man holds the woman he loves.

"Anyway—'' Drew's chest expanded as he took a deep breath "—it got me pondering the future. I used to think I had to work in the big arena—you know what I mean?''

She nodded, eager to know where this was headed.

"For the first time it occurred to me that I might be happy staying in Port Carling, keeping up the old *Gazette*. I wouldn't have to give up every part of my career....''

Oh, she couldn't believe it! Was he serious? Was this really happening? "You'd keep the radio program," she said cautiously. There had to be a catch.

No way would Drew Driscoll really stay in Port Carling.

"Sure. And I could handle the odd assignment."

He didn't sound so sure about that, though. She peered at him, trying to gauge his emotions. "The decision wouldn't be irrevocable," she pointed out.

He had no comment on that point, but his gaze slid down to her belly. "How's the baby?" he asked, reaching out to touch the firm roundness under her blouse.

"Fine. Good." He was letting his hand linger against the silky fabric, obviously unaware what his touch did to her these days. She avoided his eyes, focusing on the silver zip of his warm down vest, swallowing when his hand began to move in a caressing circle, before sliding to the small of her back.

It was happening again. One of those sharp, intense moments when all she could think about was how it had felt to have Drew make love to her.

"Mallory?" His voice had softened and deepened. When she still wouldn't look at him, he caught her chin with his fingers and raised her face a couple of inches.

"Something's gone wrong between us, hasn't it? You don't seem to want to spend as much time with me. Are you getting tired of having me around? Have I been making a nuisance of myself?"

"Never." She'd put too much feeling in that

word. Damn. She swallowed and wondered just how much she'd revealed. She ought to crack a joke of some sort to lighten the mood, but her brain was stalled.

"I'm glad." He put his other arm around her back and pulled her close. "Because I like being with you, Mal. When I'm not at work, it's you I want to be with."

Oh, what was he saying? She could feel her bones giving way; her whole body was about to melt into his.

"How's that lower back?" he whispered. "Need a little massage?" He began the rolling action with his thumbs that Stacey had taught him. It still tickled. The urge to laugh brought a welcome relief from tension.

"Drew, we're going to be the prenatal-class drop-outs."

"No, we aren't. We just need more practice."

"Really?" She didn't know how, but at some point her hands had moved to his shoulders. Now she had no choice but to look him in the eyes—and was confounded by what she saw there.

He was going to kiss her.

"Just what kind of practice do you have in mind?" she asked.

CHAPTER THIRTEEN

"YOU TELL ME. What should we practice?" Drew linked his arms behind Mallory's back and pulled her even closer, until her full breasts grazed the front of his down vest.

She didn't answer. Her moss-colored eyes looked glazed, like a pond after winter's first freeze. Drew wondered if he'd taken leave of his senses. Why was he touching her like this? There was nothing "friendlike" about his hands running the length of her back, or his pelvis automatically pressing forward at the feel of her belly.

He bent to the soft curve of her ear. "Should we practice our breathing?" He took air in and then blew gently, a quieter, more seductive version of the technique they'd learned at the prenatal class.

Mallory's eyes fluttered closed, and his throat went dry.

What was he doing? As if he didn't remember what had happened the last time he'd kissed Mallory this way. They'd ended up making love. She'd gotten pregnant. Now everything was different, and so much more complicated.

He couldn't kiss her just because he felt like it. Or because she had skin that glowed, and freckles that danced, and hair that reminded him of ripe wheat in fall.

Consequences. He had to consider consequences.

Yet hadn't he made up his mind on the drive back from Toronto? He was going to be the publisher of the *Gazette*. An image of his name under a major national front-page story came and quickly went. He'd covered some fine stories in his time—shouldn't that be enough?

He was going to stay. From there, kissing Mallory was such a logical step—and something he'd wanted to do for a long time....

He felt a stillness in her body that conjured up the metal Slinky they'd played with as children. In his mind he saw it poised on the edge of the top stair at his house, just waiting for a tiny push to go bouncing down the steps.

She was like that Slinky. All she needed was the touch of his lips and she'd be alive in his arms. He just knew it.

"Or we could practice kissing." He brushed his lips along the skin from her ear to her cheek.

"I don't think that's in the curriculum."

Was she telling him to stop? But she'd tilted her head toward him, and her hands had moved from his shoulders to his back. She seemed to want him to move even closer.

"It's in *my* curriculum," he assured her. Her lips were moist and inviting. Surely pale apricot was the most delicious color he'd ever seen.

"Mine, too." She opened her eyes for a second before he lowered his mouth to hers, and then it was exactly as he'd guessed. Her hands pressed into his back and her mouth parted sweetly.

She was uncoiling faster than he'd imagined, and he was having no difficulty keeping up.

He supported the back of her head with one hand, while with the other he drew her waist to him. He needed her close as he explored her sweetness, the details of which were slowly coming back to him, like forgotten fragments of a forbidden dream.

"I guess I was wrong." He pulled back, breathless, amazed, confounded. "We don't seem to need any practice after all."

She flashed a smile. "No. I'd say we pretty much got it right."

Drew steadied himself with a hand on either side of her hips. One kiss was not supposed to do this to a man. He had to get a grip. Make sure he hadn't read the situation wrong.

"Was I out of line?"

There was just a fraction of a pause before she replied, "You were absolutely in line."

He couldn't stop from grinning. "You, too." But now what? He felt a sliver of trepidation. Maybe he should have given this more thought before he kissed her.

But hell, several months ought to be enough.

"Don't mull it over too long," Mallory said, putting a hand to his lips.

"That's the kind of good advice a man doesn't get often enough. If I shouldn't think, what should I do?"

"Order a pizza. Rent a movie. It is Friday, after all."

And what about after the pizza, after the movie? He was almost afraid to think the questions, let alone ask them.

"WHAT WAS YOUR FAVORITE SCENE?" Drew inquired many hours later at Mallory's. He'd rented another romantic comedy, even though he'd come across a legal thriller that looked enticing. Getting the comedy instead had been worth it, though, to see that goofy smile on Mallory's face and to catch the occasional tear sliding down her cheek.

They were sitting on the couch, their feet propped up on the coffee table beside the pizza box. Inside lay the single remaining slice, the cheese wrinkled, the veggies limp. It was so unappetizing that even Doug, who was curled on the floor beside Drew, had stopped eyeing the box longingly.

Mallory was wearing baggy gray sweatpants and an old gray T-shirt with a hole at the hem. It was almost as though she'd dressed that way to discourage any further sexual thoughts on his part, but if that was her intention, then her strategy hadn't worked. Ever since he'd walked in the door, he'd been aware of her womanly body, the natural beauty of her face.

"My favorite scene? I'd have thought that was obvious."

"In the park? At the end?"

She nodded. "When Katherine finally realizes he's the one she's been in love with all along. It's just so romantic."

And completely unrealistic, Drew mused, but didn't say. Instead, he nodded. "I know what you mean."

"You do not, you fraud."

She laughed and punched him gently in the arm. He reached out quickly to capture her hand before she could withdraw it.

"I've been doing a lot of 'not' thinking about what happened this afternoon."

"That's good. I think."

"And I want to do it again. Just to make sure it wasn't a fluke." He put her hand next to his chest so she could feel how fast his heart was beating. So she might have some idea how badly he wanted her.

"It probably was a fluke. You probably can't kiss that nicely again."

"Oh, you *are* a witch." He pulled her to him,

then fell back against the arm of the couch. She landed on top of him and squirmed until she was resting on her side, facing him. He had to keep his hand on her back to prevent her from rolling off.

"Yes," she agreed. "But I'm a very good witch."

"Really?" Those lips were such a temptation. "Why don't you show me?"

SOMEHOW, THEY ENDED UP on a quilt on the floor. Mallory was lying on her back, and he was propped up on his elbow, watching her.

He took in the length and curves of her body, stopping at the mound of her belly. Gently, he lifted the bottom of her T-shirt so he could see the full rounded shape of her.

"Your tummy feels so firm." That had amazed him from the beginning. He'd expected it to be mushy.

"Claire told me Kirk finds her sexy when she's pregnant. Can you believe that?"

"Six months ago, no. Now—definitely."

Apricot flush highlighted Mallory's cheekbones; she pushed against his chest half-heartedly. "Don't mock me, Drew."

"Mal, I couldn't be more sincere." And he was more than ready to prove it to her.

Holding her gaze, he pulled the T-shirt higher to reveal the swollen mounds of her breasts. The sight stole his breath, even hidden as they were under a utilitarian beige maternity bra.

"Wow." Great. He sounded like a schoolboy.

She laughed softly. "I always wondered what it would feel like to be stacked."

"Now you know." He couldn't tear his eyes away, but she didn't seem to mind. She swallowed as he unhooked the clasp of her bra and slowly removed the cotton barrier from her skin.

Her breasts, their nipples dark and erect, cascaded from their confines. Reaching out to catch them in his hands, he felt a grinding ache in his loins.

"You are so beautiful. And desirable. Couldn't you tell how hard it's been for me to keep my hands off you?"

Her eyes lowered. "Come on, Drew. I've seen the women you've dated."

"I haven't thought about one of those women since I left Ottawa." He bent his head to catch her eye. It was important that she believe him on this. Mallory was so special there was no one like her.

"I'm happy to hear that." Tentatively, she reached for a button on his shirt.

He couldn't believe how that small move on her part ignited him. His tension mounted as she continued to the next button and the next. Finally, when his shirt lay puddled on the quilt, he reached for her, desperate to feel the softness of her breasts against his lips.

"Lie back, Mal. It's my turn now."

HIS CONTROL SNAPPED the moment Mallory called out his name, her fingers digging into his back, her pelvis rocking against his.

"Yes, Drew," Mallory urged, encouraging him. "Let it go…"

The vortex of desire sucked him under. His thrusting became faster, harder. Would he hurt her?

But no—her body rose to meet his. "Yes, Drew. Yes."

Yes. The word drove him over the edge. Yes, yes, he needed this, longed for it—

Suddenly, the seed exploded from his body, and the shock waves drove through his every nerve ending. He felt her legs clenched around him, her hands caressing his hair, his cheek, the length of his back.

Shifting his weight to the side, he held her close so they could remain linked for at least a few minutes longer. At some point they'd moved to her bed. Now he pulled the covers over her naked body.

"Are you okay?" His words came out in gasps.

"Better than okay." She brushed her hair out of her face. He'd removed the elastic, and the springy curls flew everywhere.

"Yeah. I know what you mean." He'd thought their first time had been pretty spectacular. But this. This had been volcanic.

"Drew?" Mallory's breath was like honey on his cheek.

"Yeah?"

"If you tell me this was a mistake, I'll kill you."

"And if you tell me I need more practice, I'll kill *you*."

She laughed and rolled away from him.

"Hey. Where're you going?" He felt cold without her. Cold and lonely.

"I'm getting some mineral water and strawberries from the fridge. I feel like celebrating."

"I feel like celebrating, too, but couldn't we celebrate by sleeping?"

He didn't think she heard him. The fridge door opened with a squeak, then came the clink of glasses. Only a minute later she was back. She'd poured the mineral water into champagne flutes, and now she handed him one. He'd no sooner propped himself into a sitting position than she fed him a red berry, then kissed him.

Consequences.

Maybe the word wasn't very romantic, but it was the one that popped into his mind.

There were things a man could do with regret and still live with himself later.

Walking away *for the second time* after making love with his best friend, who was now pregnant with *his* child, was not one of them.

"Will you marry me, Mal?"

HIS QUESTION LANDED in the night air like a pebble
tossed into a lake. It seemed to Mallory she could
see the ripples following one another endlessly to
the limits of her imagination.

"Will I marry you?"

Whatever she'd expected, it hadn't been this. The
events of the day were almost too much. First, he'd
told her he was staying in Port Carling. Then they'd
made love. Now this.

She felt his arm circle her waist as he waited for
her to reply.

It should have come instantly. It would have if
she'd had only her heart to consider. She propped
her head on her hand and looked at him closely.
"Are you sure, Drew?"

Drew appeared annoyed at the question. "If you
don't want to marry me, Mallory, just say so."

"I don't want you asking me because you feel
obliged. Because of the baby." She pulled back, trying to prepare herself for his answer.

"Well, I don't deny the baby is a factor. Of
course it is. But I love you more than anyone else
in the world. And obviously we've been repressing
some great chemistry over the years. Baby, love,
sex. That sounds like marriage to me, Mal. What
about you?"

She kept looking at him. He was saying all the
right things. Or was he? Somehow, something was
missing. But what?

Then he leaned forward to kiss the corner of her mouth, nuzzling his chin against hers. Mallory relaxed into the intimate touch.

She must be crazy to hesitate. This was Drew, the only man she'd ever loved, the only man she ever *could* love. And he was asking her to marry him.

"It seems like heaven to me," she said.

"Can I take that as a yes?"

"You can."

DREW KISSED MALLORY AGAIN, telling himself he'd done the right thing. She felt so good in his arms, and that was *his* baby in her belly.

Suddenly, she sat up. "I'm overwhelmed, Drew. In less than twelve hours you tell me you're staying in Port Carling, then you ask me to marry you."

He tilted his head to one side, trying to gauge her shift in mood. "This isn't a preamble to you changing your mind, is it?"

"No. Of course not." She wavered for a moment. "I guess this means I can throw away that card my customer from Toronto gave me this afternoon."

"Sorry? I'm not following."

"After you left, a man came into the shop to buy a gift for his wife's birthday. It was so sweet. He'd driven all the way from Toronto because she had her heart set on a sweater she'd noticed last fall. Fortunately, I still had it in stock."

"Yeah?"

"Anyway, I had a copy of the *Hub of the Lakes Gazette* on the counter, and he started reading it while I rang in the sale. He said he and his wife had been thinking of moving to a small town and buying a newspaper and did I know who owned the *Gazette.*"

"And you said, 'No, I've never met the man…'"

Mallory laughed. "I took his card and told him I'd give it to you. It's sitting on the night table beside you."

Drew glanced over his shoulder, and there it was, an innocuous white rectangle, lying next to the digital alarm clock and the bowl of strawberries.

That could have been my ticket out of here. With the paper sold, his family's legacy to the town would have been secured and he could have returned to Ottawa in good conscience. He could have held on to Angie's house as a rental property. As for Doug, maybe Grady or Mallory would have kept him.

"Drew?" Mallory's eyes were round with concern. "Do you want to give that guy a call?"

Guilt seared his gut. How could he have even thought those things? He loved Mallory and she needed him. Their *baby* needed him.

"Of course not, Mal. Throw the card away. I won't be using it."

CHAPTER FOURTEEN

A FEW WEEKS AFTER Drew asked her to marry him, Mallory was driving home from the Conroys', just past nine in the evening. She'd had dinner with Terese and Lisa; Drew had begged off, claiming he was knee-deep in some research at the office. Now, passing the newspaper building, she noticed a light still burning.

She pulled into a parking stall directly in front of the two-story-clapboard structure. Five years ago Angie had commissioned a new sign for the building from a local artist; it was swinging from its wrought-iron mooring, the old-fashioned lettering proclaiming Hub Of The Lakes Gazette and, in smaller letters below, Founded In 1936 By Andrew Driscoll.

Mallory stopped to look at the sign for a moment before tapping on the window. Cupping her hands to the glass, she could see Drew at his desk in the front of the office. He'd been concentrating on his computer monitor, but at the sound of her knock, he looked up. Recognizing her, he smiled and stood to open the locked door.

"What are you doing out so late?" He glanced

automatically at her stomach, as so many people seemed to do lately, and placed a protective hand on her shoulder. "Shouldn't you be at home resting?"

"I had a nap this afternoon." She was large enough now that sleeping was becoming a problem. Generally, she found it easier to take catnaps than to try for eight consecutive hours.

"I was on my way home from Terese's when I saw the light. Are you working on a story?"

He was the one who appeared tired. There were fine red lines in the whites of his eyes and his dark hair was spiked and disheveled. Even the forest-green V-necked sweater he wore over his plain white T-shirt was rumpled.

All of which only made him look sexier. Mallory brushed back his hair, allowing her hand to graze the two-day growth along his cheek. He smiled, but his eyes didn't connect with hers and his kiss was short and distracted.

"I was on the Internet, checking out some old issues of the *Globe*."

"Researching a story?" She walked over to the monitor and stood behind him when he sat down.

"Researching my life," was his dry response.

That was when she noticed the date of the article on the screen. December 1962. Drew had been born in August of 1963.

"December would have been the month you were conceived."

"That's right."

"Are you searching for information about your father?"

"Yes. I've been checking bylines, hunting for a story that might have been his. Angie said the man she was involved with was a journalist from the States. I figured that whatever story he was working on could have been picked up by the *Globe*."

Mallory watched as columns flashed by on the monitor. In all the years they'd been friends, she couldn't remember Drew expressing any curiosity about his father. This new interest—had it arisen because of Angie's death? Or because he was about to become a father himself?

"This is getting me nowhere." Drew moved the mouse impatiently, disconnecting from the Internet. He swiveled in his chair to face her, cocking his head to one side.

"Is it possible your father was someone other than that journalist?"

"I don't think so. According to Angie's friends, she was pretty focused on work and her career. Before the journalist, Buddy Conroy was her boyfriend, but they stopped seeing each other when she left Port Carling."

Drew had told Mallory about the romance, but Buddy had been married to Patricia for so many years it was hard to imagine him interested in another woman.

Now Drew got out of his chair and went to the file cabinet beside the desk. He pulled out a packet of letters, held together by a thick elastic, and passed them to her.

Mallory held them to the light, noting the Toronto address and the yellowed condition of the paper. "Are these from Buddy?"

"Yeah."

"Have you read them?"

"No. It didn't feel right. What do you think?"

Mallory gazed at the envelopes in her hand. She was curious to know how the love affair had ended. But it wasn't really any of their business.

"I think you're right, Drew. This is Buddy and Angie's story."

"Funny thing is, I tried to give the letters back to Buddy. You know what he said?"

"What?"

"To burn them. That at his age there was no sense in saving old love letters."

"I guess he figured Patricia wouldn't appreciate that." Good thinking on Buddy's part. Mallory knew how she'd feel if Drew kept souvenirs of past love affairs.

Mallory replaced the packet of letters in the file cabinet. She sensed Drew wasn't ready to get rid of them yet. If only Angie were here to answer some of his questions. But she wasn't, and she never would be.

And Drew was not the type to let sleeping dogs lie. He was a journalist, after all, trained to get to the truth of the matter.

"At least our baby will know who his father is," Drew said, coming up from behind and wrapping his arms around her bulky waist.

Mallory knew she ought to be glad that Drew was so eager to be a part of this baby's life. But she worried about the implications. She'd never understood how badly Drew wanted to find his father. Maybe that had influenced his decision to stay in Port Carling. And his decision to propose to her.

"I CAN'T BELIEVE you're eight months pregnant already!" Claire stepped back to get a better look as Mallory removed her long overcoat.

Mallory stood sideways, showcasing her tummy. "Believe it. Four weeks to go, according to the doctor. Drew and I have finished prenatal classes, and my bag for the hospital is packed."

Claire and the girls had arrived last night for a four-day weekend, and already the cottage had a warm, lived-in feeling. It was past nine o'clock so the girls were in bed, but a fire crackled in the hearth, and toys and books were scattered around. On the coffee table, Claire had a fondue pot of melted chocolate, with fresh strawberries and slices of pineapple for dipping.

Mallory settled, with only a little difficulty, on the floor beside the fondue pot. "This looks totally decadent."

"You bet. We're talking Belgian chocolate here. Dig in." Claire joined her on the floor and picked up her own fondue fork. She speared a piece of pineapple, then dipped it into the dark melted chocolate.

"Wouldn't a cup of full-bodied coffee be wonderful with this chocolate?" Mallory sighed. "Oh, well. Part of the sacrifices of being a mother, I guess."

"Honey, giving up coffee and alcohol are just the beginning, believe me. Next on the agenda comes sleep, soon it'll be all you think about."

"And after that…?"

"Well, then you start talking funny. Referring to yourself in the third person and speaking in a high-pitched voice—'Mommy said not to poke the knitting needle in your sister's ear, sweetheart.' Before you know it, you're playing Candy Land and thinking you're having a good time."

"Do you always make sure you lose when you play with your girls, Claire? I was reading that winning at games can help build a child's self-esteem."

Claire's eyes widened in feigned shock. "Didn't I warn you about those parent manuals? I used to let my girls win all the time, until I heard them talking to the neighborhood kids about my learning disability. 'She doesn't even know how to count her Monopoly money,' I heard Daisy say once.''

Mallory grabbed for a napkin so she wouldn't spurt melted chocolate over the room as she laughed. ''You're too funny, Claire.''

''It's true. I swear. But forget kids and motherhood. How did we start on that topic? I want to hear about Drew. I can't believe you two are finally getting married.''

''Why do you say 'finally'?''

''Because you belong together. And of course you've been in love with him forever.''

Of course? Mallory stirred the pot of melted chocolate with a spear of pineapple. ''I had a crush. I'll grant you that.''

''A crush? Get real. Think about the men you've dated. Did your feelings for any of them ever come close to the feelings you have for Drew?''

''That's not a fair question.''

''It is so. You just don't want to answer it. You want to know Grady's theory?''

''Excuse me?'' Mallory didn't know whether to be annoyed or amused. ''You and Grady have discussed my love life?''

Claire didn't even look abashed. ''Haven't you and I discussed Grady's? Anyway, he thinks you purposely date men you know won't measure up to Drew.''

"Come on, Claire. *You've* been reading too many relationship manuals."

"What if I have? You can't deny you've always loved Drew. And right from the start, I figured he was the father of your baby."

"You did?" So far they'd kept the news of their engagement pretty low-key. And they certainly hadn't made any announcements about paternity.

"Of course I did. Don't think I can't count backward just because I can't add Monopoly money. I checked my calendar and everything pointed to that weekend you went hiking with Drew in the Gatineau Hills. Or should I say, the weekend you *didn't* go hiking with Drew?"

Mallory shook her head, smiling ruefully.

"But back to this marriage thing. How did he propose? Did he get down on bended knee?"

"I can't remember the details, Claire." Which was a lie, of course. Mallory remembered every second of that night they'd spent together. Everything had been so perfect. Claire was so right when she said they belonged together.

And yet...

Was Drew marrying her for the right reasons? Yes, he loved her. She didn't doubt that. But did he love her the way she loved him? The other night, when she'd stopped by his office, had his world lit up when she'd walked in the door? Had the sound of her voice made his toes curl and his heart quiver? The way his did hers?

"You don't want to tell me," Claire said. "Okay. I can accept that. But what about the wedding? When are you having it?"

"Not till after the baby's born. I want to walk down the aisle at my regular weight—or something reasonably close to it. I also want Andie, Daisy and Jenna to be my flower girls. And you to be my matron of honor."

Talking with Claire made the wedding plans suddenly feel real. In a few months she and Drew would be married. It truly was going to happen.

Just a few months ago Mallory hadn't even allowed herself to dream of the possibility; now it seemed she was to be granted all her heart's desires. A child and a husband—instant family.

She should have been ecstatic. And she was. Almost. She was just being silly. Drew had asked her to marry him. That should be enough to prove how he really felt.

ON MONDAY, AFTER SCHOOL, Warren and Taylor brought their photos and a story covering the weekend hockey game into the *Gazette* offices.

"Nice work, guys." Drew sat back in his chair, feeling a warm rumble of satisfaction. Giving this job to the boys had been one of his best gambles ever. Far from letting him down, as he'd feared, they'd made every deadline and gotten some of the best pictures the newspaper had ever printed.

Warren, it turned out, was a natural with the camera, while words just seemed to flow whenever Taylor sat in front of a keyboard. Plus, Grady said they were keeping better hours, not staying out so late on the weekends.

Except they still weren't getting along with their mother very well. Hell, neither was Grady. Drew didn't know whose fault that was.

"Thanks a lot, guys. You're doing one hell of a job. Ever thought of this as a career?"

To his surprise, both boys became bashful.

"Well, we are thinking about it," Taylor said. "There's a new guidance counselor at our school, and she's been doing some testing. Journalism came up high for me."

"I'm not surprised."

The new guidance counselor would be Terese Balfour, of course. How well how her life had turned around still gratified Drew enormously.

"Can you guys cover the play-offs this spring?" he asked.

"That depends on whether Dad will drive us to the games. Mom's started selling this makeup gunk now and she's out most nights."

"Did she quit her job in Barrie?"

"No. She's still doing that, too." Warren looked

disgusted. "It's like she can't stand to be in the house anymore. She'll do anything to get away."

Drew heard the hurt child behind Warren's angry words. That Bess would want to cultivate her own interests now that her kids were older was natural. But was it possible she'd gone overboard?

"Well, if your dad can't drive you, I'm always available." Or at least he would be until the baby was born.

What would life be like then? Part of him was excited by the prospect. But part of him was worried, too. Would he be any good at being a father, at living permanently in a small town like Port Carling, at being a husband?

Would stories like the one he'd done on Terese Balfour and her child continue to provide him with the sort of satisfaction he needed from his work?

"Then we'll do it," Warren said, confirming his verbal decision with a glance at his brother. He tapped the check Drew had given him on the edge of the desk. "See you next week."

"You bet."

Drew smiled, but once they were gone, the corners of his mouth pulled down.

This morning he'd stopped by Mallory's before work to tell her he would be doing a profile on the new minister of their church. Should he book their wedding date at the same time?

He'd thought it was a practical suggestion, but

she'd balked at setting a date. Now that they were making love on a regular basis, their relationship had an added intimacy, but he felt that she was still holding herself back somehow.

It made him wonder if she really loved him or if she'd just talked herself into marriage to give their baby a father. That was just the sort of thing Mallory would do.

CHAPTER FIFTEEN

ALL THE PRENATAL CLASSES in the world could never prepare you for the real birth of a baby, Drew realized on the night of April 11.

Mallory's contractions were coming five minutes apart when they decided it was time to go to the hospital. Of course it had to be the day they were hit with a freak snowstorm, the kind where each snowflake carried the equivalent of about one cup's worth of water.

Drew shoveled out the drive while Mallory grabbed her bag, then he set out extra food for Doug. He'd already called Grady, who'd agreed to look in on the old retriever in the morning.

"Ready?" He held open the door as Mallory eased into the passenger seat. "Thank God you had the good sense to buy an all-wheel-drive vehicle."

"The highways will be clear, Drew." Mallory's voice sounded small as she tried to reassure him. She was as scared as he was. Probably more, given that the baby had to come out of *her* body.

As it turned out, the highways were *not* clear, and just staying on the road was a challenge. Plus, the hypnotic effect of millions of snowflakes cascading down on his windshield made him feel as if he were flying a spaceship through the galaxy at warp speed.

"It's okay," he kept repeating, whether to reassure Mallory or himself, he wasn't sure. Mallory didn't say anything, just kept reaching into her purse for yet another tissue. She'd caught a cold a day ago and had been too stuffed up to sleep well last night. It didn't look as though she'd be sleeping much tonight, either.

"Are you nervous, Mal?" he asked when they finally pulled into the parking lot at the Bracebridge Hospital. The contractions were still five minutes apart, so maybe there was no reason to panic.

"Yes," she said as he took her arm to guide her to the admitting room. Fortunately, they'd toured the hospital as part of their prenatal classes, so he knew where to go, what to do.

Still, it took half an hour before they were settled into a room.

"Do you want a massage, Mal? Should we practice our breathing?" He was going to do this right, to help her any way he could.

But she just laughed. "Relax, Drew. This is a piece of cake. Maybe we came down here for nothing. I don't think anything's happening."

An hour later, the situation was totally reversed.

"Get me pain relief, Drew," Mallory demanded, her hand gripping his forearm. "Or you'll never type another news story in your life.'' She twisted his arm mercilessly, and he struggled not to gasp. ''Do you understand?'' she added.

''Yes, Mallory.'' He looked into the gray eyes of the presiding nurse, and she nodded knowingly.

''We'll have the anesthesiologist up here shortly.''

''Define 'shortly,''' Mallory rasped as another contraction hit her.

Drew offered her ice, as the prenatal instructor had suggested, but Mallory brushed him away. This wasn't going the way it had on the video they'd watched, and he was concerned. Especially when he heard two nurses conferring about Mallory's body temperature.

''She's spiking a fever.'' One of them turned to him. ''Was she ill when she came in?''

''She has a cold,'' he said, wishing Mallory could call in sick. *Sorry, can't have labor right now. Call me later when I'm feeling better.*

But this baby was having none of that. He was coming tonight.

At four in the morning, the doctor decided Mallory's cervix was almost fully dilated. Time to move into the birthing room. Drew donned protective clothing and followed Mallory into a larger, sterile-looking room.

When I come out of here, I'm going to be a father, he told himself.

But the baby was still inside Mallory, and it seemed unbelievable that he'd get out.

The epidural had given Mallory quite a bit of relief, but it was wearing off and the contractions were putting her through agony.

"That's good, though," one nurse tried to tell her. "You'll be able to push harder."

"Push?" Mallory looked on the verge of tears. "I don't have enough energy to breathe."

Drew took her hand. It felt warm. Too warm. He brushed her forehead—it was really hot. *She's too sick to do this,* he wanted to say. But there was nothing anyone could do.

"It won't be long now," the doctor assured them. "This baby is ready to come out. See? He's crowning."

Cautiously, Drew peered behind the mound of green hospital sheets. "Oh, my God." He could see matted brown hair. That was the baby.

"Mallory, his head is showing."

But she didn't hear him. She was pushing and straining, listening to the commands of the nurse standing on the other side of the bed from Drew.

"That's it, sweetheart," the nurse was saying. "You're doing great. Take a deep breath and push for a good twenty seconds. Here, I'll count..."

Drew's fingers were crunched under Mallory's grip. He willed her to keep pushing, to concentrate on each tiny puff of air she expelled.

"Yes, Mallory, yes. You can do it."

"I can't!" she cried, but she already had.

"We've got her," the doctor announced triumphantly. "Your new baby daughter. She's pink and healthy, and raring to go."

That was when Drew realized that small mewing sound was his daughter's first cry. He turned to Mallory. She was lying against her pillow, exhausted, her cheeks unnaturally pink.

"You're amazing, Mallory." He stroked the top of her head, brushing back her frizzy hair and wondering where she'd found the strength.

Now the nurse gave Mallory the baby, placing her on Mal's chest. The tiny thing was still waxy and damp, and the nurse encouraged Mallory to breastfeed.

"Oh, Drew. She's beautiful."

"Yes. And so are you." He kissed her hot forehead and caressed her cheek.

"Let's name her Angelina—for your mother." Mallory looked up at him as their baby began to nurse. "Angel. Do you like that, Drew?"

Somehow, his throat had choked up. He thought of his mother, and wished she could have seen her granddaughter. Just once.

"Angel. I like it." And the amazing thing was, this teeny bit of humanity seemed exactly that. An angel. Even with hardly any hair and her head misshapen from the birth canal, she was perfect. Absolutely perfect.

He held out his finger to her tiny hand and was amazed when she grabbed on and clutched with all her might.

He lost his heart forever then, and knew he'd do anything to protect Angel from all the injustices, all the pain this world had to offer.

MALLORY COULDN'T REMEMBER feeling so weak and tired in her life. They kept her in the hospital for several days, until her fever subsided. When she arrived home she was still exhausted, and a little unsure of her ability to cope.

"Let me move into the spare room and help you out for a while," Drew offered.

"Would you?" She felt so relieved. Her first night back in her own bed was wonderful. Angel went down around one in the morning, and for the first time ever Mallory crawled between the sheets without washing her face or brushing her teeth.

She burrowed her arms under her pillow and curled up on her left side. The house was quiet; Drew had fallen asleep on the couch after hours of pacing back and forth with the baby. Within seconds Mallory was asleep, too, lost to a slumber so heavy it felt drug induced.

The next thing she heard was a thin high-pitched wail. At first she didn't remember where she was or what could be making that sound. She tried to lift her head and open her eyes. The struggle back to consciousness was like swimming through molasses. She would have given up except for the urgent sense that she had something important to do.

That wailing. It just would not stop. Then everything clicked into place, and she remembered her baby. She had to get up to feed her. Mallory needed all her willpower to lift her head from the pillow and turn around.

But by then Drew was in the doorway. His hair was going in all directions his chin was rough with an unshaven beard. He looked as exhausted as she felt, yet his expression as he gazed at the babe he held against his naked chest was soft and loving.

"Okay, Angel," he crooned. "Here's your mama." He sat on the edge of Mallory's bed while she propped herself up with several pillows.

Eyes barely open, Mallory lifted the side of her T-shirt and fumbled with the flap of her maternity bra. When one swollen nipple finally emerged, Drew handed her the baby.

"Thank you, Drew," she mumbled, before realizing that he had already gone. She nursed Angel for ten minutes on one side, then saw that the sprite had fallen asleep again.

She readjusted her bra and pulled down her shirt. Shifting the covers to the side, she was about to swing out of bed, when Drew magically reappeared.

"That's okay, Mal. I'll change her and put her in her crib. You get a little more rest."

What about you? She didn't manage to say the words before he was gone again, and she was too tired to go in pursuit. Thankful, she let her head fall back on the pillow.

Then all was dark and silent once more.

DREW TOOK CARE OF EVERYTHING that first week home. Meals and laundry, diapers and baths. Mallory felt positively spoiled. He brought Angel to her when she needed feeding and carried her away to burp and change her when they were done.

She was recovering her strength, and most of her good humor, by the beginning of the second week. That Drew had managed to find time to write his editorial and make sure the weekly edition of the *Gazette* went out on schedule, as well as hold things together at the house, amazed her.

"You are incredible, do you know that?" she said one afternoon while she was nursing Angel for what seemed like the tenth time that day.

"Listen to this." He folded over the top pages of the *Gazette,* then read:

"Mallory Lombard and Drew Driscoll are thrilled to announce the safe arrival of Angelina Jane, weighing seven pounds, seven ounces, on April 12, at 6:21 a.m. Angel took the world by storm, arriving along with record levels of snow for the area.''

"Oh, Drew." She hadn't thought of putting an announcement in the paper, but of course he would have. Now he looked so pleased with himself, and the truth was, she was pleased, too. He'd taken public responsibility for this baby. It was a good sign for the future.

Or was it? Since the moment of Angel's birth, Mallory had felt not the slightest doubt that Drew shared the same overpowering love that she did. For Angel.

But what about his feelings for her? Was it her imagination, or was he avoiding her when the baby wasn't around?

"Look. She's sleeping."

Mallory lowered her gaze to the infant. Angel's eyelashes were splayed against her chubby little cheeks, even though her tiny mouth was still pursed around Mallory's nipple.

"I'll put her down for you." As Drew reached out his arms, Mallory scrutinized him. She saw the way he kept his eyes averted from her naked breast.

"That's okay," she said. "I'm feeling better now. It's time I started pulling my weight around here." She carried her daughter to the baby room, which Therese had painted in pastels while Mallory was in the hospital.

Mallory settled Angel in the crib, swallowing the lump that always settled in her throat when she saw her baby sleeping.

A few seconds later she heard Drew's quiet steps behind her.

"Is she still asleep?" He peered in from the doorway.

"I think so." Mallory crept from the room, half-closing the door behind her. "Want to sit out on the deck and have a drink?"

"I thought maybe you'd want to take a nap. I can do the lunch dishes and the laundry...."

"Oh, to heck with the chores." Mallory spoke with a lightness she definitely did not feel. "It's such a nice afternoon. Let's relax for a minute."

"I guess."

She went into the kitchen and poured iced tea into two tall glasses, then handed him one. He took it with a resigned sigh, which only stirred the anxiety overtaking her.

What was going on in that man's mind? Did he have any idea how unhappy he looked right now?

Outside, the midday sun was warm on the weathered cedar. Mallory sank into a chair, wondering what to do. She'd never imagined the atmosphere between her and Drew could be this strained. It was as if they had nothing to say to each other.

"You've been the greatest help, Drew. I really

appreciate your having stayed here to give me a hand.''

"Hey, she's my baby, too." The comment was light, but dark undertones colored the look he gave her. "Any particular reason for using the past tense?''

Mallory folded her long skirt around her legs. "I just assumed you'd be moving back to Angie's house once I was feeling better." Her appetite had returned; she wasn't as tired as she had been. All that remained of her cold was a lingering dry cough.

"I see." Drew's knuckles turned white against the dark blue of his glass. "You mean until we're married?''

Married? Mallory pressed her lips together, not wanting them to tremble. Maybe the stress of having a new baby was making Drew so unusually withdrawn, but she doubted it. Whenever he held Angel he appeared so happy, so at peace.

The problem had to be her. She averted her gaze and took a gulp of the ice-cold beverage, then let her eyes slide back to him. He was staring at the cedar decking, his legs apart, his glass cupped in his hands.

What was he thinking? If only she could trust him to tell her what was really in his heart. But she knew that as long as he thought she wanted to get married, he would never let her down.

"Sure," she said. "Until the wedding."

DREW GLANCED UP from the shopping channel to see the light go on in Angel's bedroom. He checked his watch. The two o'clock feeding. Angel had settled like clockwork into her routine, even though she was only three weeks old.

Drew turned back to the television, wishing he were still in the spare bedroom at Mallory's, helping out the way he had that first week.

He missed that constant interaction with his daughter, the feeling of being needed and important. Now he was a guest. Someone who visited from time to time but wasn't a mainstay in her life.

Of course, this living apart wasn't going to last forever. Soon, he and Mallory would be married and the three of them would be a real family then.

The glib answer brought him no relief.

Marrying Mallory had seemed the perfect answer only months ago. Indeed, now that Angel was on the scene, marriage seemed pretty much inescapable.

Inescapable. His choice of word seemed to sum up the whole story, didn't it? Not that he didn't love Mallory. He did. But something had changed between them. He felt so uncomfortable around her, and ashamed of his sexual desires when she was still recovering physically from the delivery.

Impatient with the parade of merchandise in front of him, Drew clicked the remote control. This time he found a movie he'd once watched with Mallory.

It was a really old flick, sappy as a maple tree in spring. Oh, he'd teased Mallory when she'd cried.

"Get real," he'd said, tickling the bottom of her feet. She'd hiccuped when her laughing mingled with her tears, then she'd planted a pillow in his face and told him to be quiet for a change.

Drew changed the channel, again and again, then finally turned the television off. The lights had gone out next door. He should try to get some sleep.

As he prepared for bed, he thought about the fun he and Mallory used to have together. The hours they'd spent talking. How no topic had ever been off bounds.

What had happened to those people? he wondered. Would they come back after the wedding? Or had they somehow gotten lost forever?

CHAPTER SIXTEEN

MALLORY WAS FOLDING a load of Angel's laundry on the kitchen table when she heard Drew tap on the back door.

She opened it for him. "Angel's already asleep for the night." She was going down around nine o'clock pretty consistently now. Claire said she was lucky, but Mallory didn't feel that lucky these days.

Angel was doing so well, but Mallory's relationship with Drew had never been worse. Every day that they avoided talking about their problems, the distance between them grew. Mallory wondered what Drew thought when he looked at himself in the mirror. Did he see that his face was becoming gaunt, that somehow his spark had gone out? And if he did, did he blame the changes on her?

"I didn't come to see Angel. I wanted to talk to you." He turned one of the chairs backward and straddled it with his long legs.

Mallory continued to fold. Here was the sleeper she'd bought when she'd first found out she was pregnant. She'd been right; Angel had looked adorable in it. But the little bears were already starting to fade and Angel was growing so quickly it would only fit her another week or two at most.

"I want to talk about us, Mal. About getting married."

Mallory smoothed down the flannel of a receiving blanket. It was so soft and comforting. She wanted to wrap it around herself and block out this conversation. But they'd been hiding from the truth for too long now.

"How can we talk about getting married, Drew, when we can't even look each other in the eye anymore?"

He glanced away from her, proving her point.

See? she wanted to say. But she didn't. It hurt too much. How had it happened? They'd been best friends for so many years. She didn't regret that they'd had a child—how could she be sorry she'd had Angel? If only she hadn't complicated matters by falling in love with him. That was how the problems had started.

"You're right," Drew said. "Things have been different between us. But we can get married and work our problems through."

"Why are you arguing for something you so obviously don't want?" Not once since Angel was born had he looked at her with the passion he'd once been barely able to contain. It wasn't just the baby's birth that had cooled his ardor, Mallory knew.

She'd made the mistake of crossing the line.

She'd gone from friend to lover. And soon she would be the same as all his other lovers. History.

"I love you, Mallory. And I love Angel."

"Then why do you look so miserable? Why don't you eat? Why are you losing sleep?" She'd noticed the glare from his television, late at night, when she was up with Angel. And anyone could see the dark smudges under his eyes.

"Hell. Why are you making this so difficult?"

"Maybe I'm just questioning your motives."

"My motives?" He burst from the chair, almost knocking it down. "I'm just trying to do what's right."

She'd been correct. He was acting out of duty. That was all there was to his oh-so-gallant offer of marriage. "What about doing what you want?"

"I haven't been able to do that since Angie died."

"And whose fault is that? Nobody asked you to do anything, Drew. You just presumed. You presumed the *Gazette* couldn't go on without you, that I couldn't survive without you. Well, maybe you're not as indispensable as you think."

"Really?"

He backed away from her, his expression a mixture of scorn and dislike. She'd never dreamed he would ever look at her that way.

"If you want to go, then go." She hid her trembling hands in a pile of blankets. "That card from the man who wanted to buy the paper is still on my bedside table. Help yourself.''

Then she picked up the blankets and headed for the linen cupboard in the bathroom.

DREW STARED AFTER HER. His stomach was heaving. He felt as though he was about to be sick.

God, he'd been a fool. Assuming that she loved him, that she needed him, when in reality she felt as trapped about getting married as he did. Hadn't she just said as much? The words still rang in his ears: *You're not as indispensable as you think.*

Slowly, he walked down the hall, past the open door that led to Angel's nursery. He wouldn't look inside. Not this time. Because just one look would break his resolve. He didn't want to leave his Angel, could hardly stand to think of a day without her in it.

When he reached the bathroom door he turned right, to Mallory's room. The bed was made, but a pile of dirty laundry lay on the floor. He avoided the tangle of T-shirts and maternity bras, and stepped over a dog-eared book on baby and child care. On the night table sat the card, just as she'd said.

He glanced down at it: Willard P. Smythe, Public Relations Director. The company name beneath was one he recognized. Angie had bought most of her computer equipment from them.

In the next room he heard a door close, the sound of running water. For some reason he remembered the first night he'd spent here, after Angie died. Waking to hear Mallory throwing up in the bathroom.

Even then she'd hidden the truth from him.

She didn't want him. And nobody needed him. Hell, even his own mother hadn't told him when she found out she had cancer.

He slammed his fist on the bedside table. Then picked up the card and put it in his pocket.

BUDDY CONROY HAD THE CONTRACT in his briefcase when he pulled up in front of the *Gazette* office on Saturday morning. His joints ached as he pushed open the front door, reminding him that he was getting old. No sense in denying it.

Drew was watching, his expression grim, but neither said a word. Not at first. Buddy placed his briefcase on Drew's desk and snapped it open. He extracted the papers, then handed them to Drew.

"I've done what you asked. Here's the contract to sell the *Gazette*. I've also got a rental agreement for the house."

Drew took the papers and started looking through them. Buddy sat down, thinking there were times when being a lawyer could be a real pain.

Not only was this new guy, Willard P. Smythe,

going to take over Angie's paper, he was moving into her house, as well. Buddy didn't like it.

Having Drew back in town had sat right. But obviously, Drew didn't agree. Nothing Buddy could do about it. This was Drew's life, and he had a right to his own decisions. Still, he felt he'd let Angie down.

"What's this all about?" Drew asked, pointing his pen at the section Buddy had taken the liberty to add.

"That's a buyback clause," Buddy said.

"I didn't request any buyback clause."

"No. I put that in on my own. I'm hoping you'll humor me, Drew. What can it hurt? You don't have to act on it if you don't want. And just in case you do change your mind..."

"I'm not going to change my mind."

Buddy was inclined to believe him. He'd never seen the boy looking so serious. "Maybe not. But sometimes closing a door too firmly behind you is a mistake."

What if Angie hadn't been so certain she would never return to Port Carling when she'd left for college? What if she'd agreed to carry on their relationship from a distance?

Not that he'd ever regretted marrying Patricia. But he was old enough to realize that happiness could come from more than one fork in the road.

"I don't know, Buddy." Drew tapped his pen impatiently on the page. "Smythe might not like this."

"I'm sure you can talk him into it."

"Yeah, you're probably right." Drew smiled briefly, then arranged the contracts in a neat stack. "I'm expecting him in a few minutes. Can I call you if I run into any problems?"

"Of course you can." Buddy stood to leave, taking his empty briefcase with him.

His footstep felt lighter, and the ache in his knee didn't seem as bad as it had a few minutes ago. He'd done what little he could; now he could only sit back and hope.

GRADY WAS IN THE DRIVEWAY washing his Jeep, when Drew walked over later that day. He'd just finished his business with Smythe and they'd celebrated with a couple of drinks, so he'd decided against driving.

"I figured you'd stop by sometime today," Grady said, dropping the cloth he'd been using to buff the side mirrors.

"You did?" Drew shoved his hands into the pockets of his jeans. It was an hour past dinnertime, but the day was still bright, thanks to the high arc cut by the June sun.

"Yeah. Mallory was talking to Claire, and Claire gave me a call…" He shrugged. "You know. The usual way information gets passed on around here."

"I know." Drew scuffed the ground with his shoe. "So you've heard it all? How I've sold the business and rented the house?"

Grady rested a hand on the Jeep's hood. "Yeah. I heard. When do you head back to Ottawa?"

"Tomorrow. I'm driving, so it'll take most of the day. A few days to settle in, then I'll be looking for a good story or two. I've been out of circulation. It might take a while."

"It'll come," Grady predicted. He leaned back against the metal and put a hand to his chin. "I've got some news, as well."

"Oh?" Drew walked a few steps closer, his first thought for the twins. But he should have known the trouble wouldn't start there.

"It's Bess. She's leaving me." Grady focused on the gravel driveway and rubbed his chin a little harder.

Drew went to stand beside him and stared at the same patch of dry, dirty rock. "Man, I'm sorry to hear that."

"Yeah." Grady shook his head. "I should have seen it coming. I guess in a way I did, but I still feel kinda in shock about it."

"When did it happen?"

"According to Bess, it's been happening for about five years." He laughed dryly. "But I found out last night. Seems she bought a town house in

Barrie. She moved out this morning. Truck'll be here tomorrow for the furniture.''

"Is she cleaning out the place?''

"No. She gave me a list of what she wanted. It looked fair, so I said go ahead. What does it matter, anyway?''

The furniture compared with Bess. No, Drew could see that loss of the furniture wouldn't amount to much. "How are the boys?''

"They tore out of here after we told them this morning.'' Grady sucked in a lungful of air. "Bess thinks it's better if they stay here with me so they don't have to change schools. I can't tell you how relieved I was to hear that. But I don't know if the boys took it the right way.''

"I'm guessing they feel their mother has abandoned them.''

"That's how I'd feel in their shoes.''

Drew thought about Bess—the new job, the new condo. "Is she? Abandoning them?''

"She says not. She says she still loves them, but they don't need her anymore. She says none of us needs her, but that just isn't true.'' Grady rubbed a sleeve over his eyes. "I don't know how she plans to spend time with them. They won't want to give up their weekends to go to her condo in Barrie.''

Drew considered how important Warren's and Taylor's friends were to them. Then there was the work the two boys did for his paper. Work they were good at and enjoyed. "No. Probably not."

"But hell." Grady picked up the rag he'd dropped and started polishing again. "You don't need to worry about our problems. You've got enough of your own."

Wasn't that the truth.

"I'm real sorry, old pal."

"Me, too, Drew. Me, too."

DREW DIDN'T PACK MUCH to take with him to Ottawa. Just his clothes, his laptop and a boxful of reference books and papers.

He was renting the house furnished. It was what he and Smythe had agreed to for the three-month trial period.

And he was taking the Explorer, of course. The only part of his inheritance that he hadn't sold. He shut the trunk and pocketed the keys, then paused to look up at the clear blue sky.

That the weather was so perfect, today of all days, didn't seem fitting. A nice steady rain would have felt about right.

In the yard next to his, Mallory was sitting on the patio, with Angel on her lap. Doug lay in the shade of the big maple. Drew had taken the dog dish and leash over a few hours ago. Now he pushed aside the raspberry bushes, which were already beginning to blossom.

"You sure about keeping Doug?"

Mallory glanced up from under her wide-brimmed straw hat. She had on a long flowered dress and had slipped her feet out of the white sandals she'd worn to church that morning. Her hair was down, and flowed around her shoulders, looking for all the world like a tumbleweed that had found a mooring.

She was about as beautiful as he'd ever seen her, but also as remote as a stranger. There was none of the warmth in her eyes that he was so used to seeing. At least not when she gazed at him.

What had happened to his best friend? God, he missed that woman, and missed even more the lover he'd discovered in the weeks before Angel's birth.

Yet hadn't he known when he'd taken Mallory into his arms that second time that he was somehow gambling everything they had together on the chance that love might work out between them?

At the time, it had seemed a chance worth taking. Now, having lost, he wondered why he couldn't have been happy with what he'd had.

"I'll be glad to watch him," Mallory said. "He's too old to move so far away. At least this is his neighborhood, and he knows me."

"Yeah." It was better for the dog to stay, but Drew would miss him. If he didn't travel so much, he'd have been tempted to take Doug anyway.

"All packed?" Mallory asked.

He nodded, his attention caught by his daughter's

blue-green eyes. Not like his, not like Mallory's, but some combination of the two.

How could he leave her, his little Angel?

Let me hold her, Mal, he wanted to say, but at the moment he couldn't speak. He'd be coming back to Port Carling soon, but how much would she have changed? Leaving now, he was giving up precious weeks. Weeks that he would never get back.

Oh, God, was he doing the right thing? Would things ever be right again?

MALLORY TOOK OFF HER HAT and lifted Angel so she could see her daughter's face. It was round and soft and completely dominated by her long-lashed eyes. The poor thing had no idea what was happening right now. But the consequences of this day would stay with her all her life.

That was the legacy Mallory had chosen to give Angel by sending Drew away.

But what choice had she had? From the beginning she'd resolved to raise this child on her own. And that was the way it was going to be.

"Do you want to say goodbye?" She held out her arms toward Drew, and he stepped forward to take his daughter.

He curled her into his elbow and clamped his lips together. Mallory felt as though her heart were burning when she caught sight of the pain in his tightly set mouth.

Drew pressed a kiss onto each of Angel's cheeks. "I'll be back, little one. You're going to be seeing a lot of me."

Mallory shifted her eyes, focusing on the back of the house. The thought of missing one day with Angel was enough to bring tears to her eyes. She couldn't fathom leaving for weeks, possibly months.

How can you go? she wanted to ask. But it was obvious this was tearing him apart, too. She felt dampness under her right eye and quickly rubbed it away.

But not without Drew noticing. He reached out to touch her arm. "I'm so sorry, Mal. You've always meant the world to me. I didn't want that ever to change."

But it had. He'd changed, and so had she. They'd have to keep seeing each other because of Angel. But they'd likely never recapture the special bond they'd always shared.

"You have a safe trip, Drew." She leaned forward to take the baby, and he kissed her cheek, pressing his hand against her hair and holding her there for several long seconds.

"I will. I'll call."

She watched him walk back to Angie's yard, to where the Explorer was packed and waiting. He was tall and sexy in his faded jeans and bleached cotton T-shirt, and leaner than ever. He slipped on a pair of sunglasses, then slid into the driver's seat.

She heard the engine start, saw him slowly back the vehicle out of the drive.

I don't want you to go. The words screamed, but only in her mind.

With a final salute, he turned to the road and never looked back.

Gone. He was gone. And her world resounded with the emptiness. She realized the baby was asleep, so she took her into the house and settled her in her crib, then went back outside. Hugging her arms to her body, she wandered the yard as poor Doug watched her nervously.

She'd been almost numb when she and Drew were saying their goodbyes. Now feeling was returning, and it was worse than she'd ever imagined. Pain, despair, heartache.

No more long, late-night conversations. No joking insults about her hair. No Friday-night pizza and videos....

Who would laugh at her when she cried during her favorite romantic comedies? Who would tell her not to worry the first time Angel fell and bumped her head? Who would give her a massage that created more aches than it relieved?

If not Drew, then no one.

"Oh God." Mallory took a breath, but all she gained were fresh barbs of pain. Suddenly panic hit. Why had she let him leave? Why hadn't she tried to stop him?

She ran out to the street, bare feet sinking on the tufts of thick grass. Maybe he would change his mind. Maybe he already turned around.

But no. The road was clear as far as she could see. He wouldn't come back, he was never coming back. At least not for her.

CHAPTER SEVENTEEN

SUMMER HOLIDAYS HIT with a blazing heat wave and a heavy blanket of humidity. Cottages around Port Carling were full once more, and traffic pulsed along Highway 400, peaking on Friday and Sunday evenings as the weekenders from Toronto raced from and to the city.

It was time for Mallory to go back to work. She took Angel into the shop for the Saturday of the July long weekend and managed to put in a five-hour shift. The staff were delighted to see her back and even more thrilled to have the opportunity to hold the baby. At the end of the day, she stopped at Marg's to get a milkshake and muffin.

She ate not out of any desire for food but because she had to. On the day Drew had left, something hard and heavy had settled in the bottom of her stomach; she was beginning to wonder if it would ever go away.

Once she'd finished eating, she strapped Angel into her infant seat in the back of the car. No sooner did she start the engine than the exhausted tyke fell asleep.

Mallory hesitated for a moment. She'd been putting off an errand far too long. Probably because she
felt so darned guilty. Bess Hogan had never been
one of Mallory's favorite people, and she knew
Claire had never liked her.

Perhaps Bess had resented being treated like an
outsider by her husband's circle of friends. Maybe
if they had made more of an effort, Bess would have
been happier.

Mallory started the car and headed resolutely for
the highway. They might never have been close, but
for more than fifteen years she'd eaten Thanksgiving
dinners with Bess and been invited to her boys'
birthday parties. She couldn't let Grady's wife move
out of town, and out of their lives, unacknowledged.

The drive to Barrie passed quickly and she had
no trouble locating Bess's new town house—Grady
had given her the address and phone number several
weeks ago.

Angel was still sleeping, so Mallory decided to
leave her in the car until she found out whether Bess
was home or not. After opening all four windows in
the vehicle, she ran up the sidewalk to the front door
of the town house.

Bess had potted flowers on the stairs, and a pretty
mat in front of the door. She seemed to have settled
right in. Mallory rang the bell.

Bess answered wearing a summery shift, her face
all made up. Her smile faded when she saw Mallory.

"I was just on my way to one of my cosmetic parties." Her gaze roamed past Mallory to her vehicle on the street. "Are you alone?"

"Angel's asleep in the car. I'm sorry to drop in without notice. It's just that I've been meaning to come and see you. I want you to know that your friends in Port Carling are thinking of you."

For a second she was certain she glimpsed tears in Bess's eyes. But then the heavily made-up lashes blinked away all signs.

"I appreciate the thought, Mallory. It was really sweet of you. However, I'm trying to start a new life for myself. I won't be keeping in touch...."

"I'm sorry to hear that, Bess. Everyone misses you." Especially Grady and the boys.

"I highly doubt that." Bess leaned against the door frame. She still hadn't asked Mallory in, and obviously had no plans to do so.

"Come on, Bess. Of course they do." And didn't *she* miss *them?* Not to mention the town she'd lived in all her life? "Did you hear that the twins aren't working for the *Gazette* anymore? The new editor decided he'd rather cover the sporting events himself."

That was a real shame, when the boys had done such a great job. But maybe it would be good if it meant they had more time to spend with their mother.

"No, I hadn't heard...."

When had Bess last talked to her sons? Mallory didn't want to judge the woman, especially when it was evident that behind her cool facade Bess was in pain. Even if she didn't want to admit it.

"They don't need me anymore, Mallory. The boys are practically grown, and Grady always was a much better father than I was a mother."

"Grady is a good dad. But that doesn't mean—"

"It's too late, Mallory. This new start is just what I need. You don't know how long I've craved the chance to do something on my own."

"But Grady and the twins—"

"Are doing just fine without me," Bess interjected. "Don't try to tell me I'm indispensable. Because I know it isn't true."

Indispensable. Now, where had she heard that word before?

Mallory drove home full of self-doubt. Perhaps it had been a mistake for her to visit Bess. She hadn't meant to try to talk the other woman into going back to her family. She'd just wanted to let her know that she still had friends in Port Carling.

But clearly Bess wasn't interested in anyone or anything from Port Carling. A new start, she'd said. Well, she was welcome to it. Still, that conclusion she'd come to about not being indispensable...

Of course Mallory remembered where and when she'd heard that word last. She'd hurled it at Drew before he'd walked out on her and Angel.

Was that the real reason he'd left? Not because he was secretly pining for his old life in Ottawa but because Mallory had made him feel unneeded?

It was a very bitter thought.

MALLORY DROVE to Claire's cottage, unable to face her own empty house. Claire and the girls had arrived for the long weekend, although they were going back to Toronto on Monday for the girls' annual two weeks of swimming lessons.

Mallory bounced Angel on her knee, smiling each time the little baby met her eyes. "Is Kirk planning to come to the cottage this summer?"

"He's taking three weeks in August. It's the longest holiday he's had in years." Claire went to the kitchen for a couple of glasses of lemonade. "I've made up my mind that this is going to be a period of renewal for the two of us and our marriage. All those quiet summer nights after the girls are asleep—what better opportunity to get to know each other again? With the hours he's been working, and after having three children back-to-back…"

Claire shrugged, setting a glass down on the table beside Mallory. "Jenna's four now. It's time we made room for the two of us again."

"I'm glad to hear it," Mallory said. There'd been too much turmoil in her friends' lives lately, her own, too. Claire's positive attitude was a welcome one.

Claire plucked Angel out of her arms and held the child close. Angel peered at the new face alertly, and Claire kissed her cheek. Then she looked at her friend again.

"I'm sorry, Mallory. I couldn't believe it when you told me Drew was moving back to Ottawa. I thought he was here for good."

Me, too. "It's not just me, Claire. Poor Grady. He's so unhappy with Bess gone. I went to see her today."

That got Claire's attention. "You did?"

"She's really settled into her new plan. She wasn't very happy to see me though."

"Any chance she'll return home? To Grady and the boys?"

"I doubt it. She seems determined to start a new life for herself. And equally eager to distance herself from anything to do with Port Carling."

Claire positioned Angel in a corner of the sofa. "Maybe it's easier for her to leave that way."

"She said they didn't need her anymore—Grady and the boys. Why would she feel that way?"

"Maybe it's her way of justifying her own actions."

"You think she wanted to leave—and just needed an excuse to move out on Grady and the boys?"

"It's possible."

It was. And maybe Drew had used the same excuse. But if he had, it was only because Mallory had given it to him. She'd let him leave believing he wasn't needed anywhere—not by her, or Angel, or even at the *Gazette*.

But just the opposite was true. She needed him so much she could hardly eat or sleep. She couldn't watch a movie without crying. And she'd probably never order another pizza in her life.

As for Angel, she was too young now, but in a few years she'd really miss not having a daddy who was part of her day-to-day life.

And the town already missed Drew. The *Gazette* was not what it had been. The tone and character of the paper had completely changed.

As if aware of her train of thought, Claire asked, "Have you heard from Drew?"

"Just once. He called the day he drove back to Ottawa."

"Nothing since?"

"Nothing."

Mallory went to stand at the window. The sun was setting now, spreading golden-orange rays over the horizon, where they reflected on the still waters of Lake Rosseau. The beauty of the sunset gave her comfort. Not everything was changing. You could still count on some things.

Like sunsets, and crowds in the store on week-ends, and friends like Claire.

Of course she'd thought that way about Drew

once, too. One year ago she'd never have believed their friendship could be shattered so irrevocably.

DREW WAITED until he'd finished preparing for his weekly radio program before he allowed himself to look at the latest copy of the *Gazette*, which had arrived in the mail that day.

He was sitting on the sofa in his living room. An open beer stood beside his feet on the coffee table, and stacks of notes lay everywhere he looked. He shoved aside the pile dealing with the radio show and picked up the *Gazette*.

This was Willard P. Smythe's fourth issue, and Drew wondered what new changes he'd find this time. He had to admit that seeing Smythe's name instead of his or Angie's on the masthead and on the editorial page had given him a jolt in the gut.

One of this week's alteration caught his eye immediately.

Smythe had changed the nameplate.

"Damn," Drew muttered. *News from the Hub of the Lakes* stood out in black capital letters in a modern font totally unlike the old-fashioned Bookman that he and his mother had preferred.

The front-page picture showed hordes of people strolling along Steamboat Bay and was captioned, "Summer back in full force."

That made him think of Mallory. Had she returned to work as planned? She must be swamped these days what with all the tourists. Did she take Angel into the store with her? What a change that would make to the little one's quiet world.

Drew flipped to the op-ed page, and literally chewed his lip as he read Smythe's editorial, which advocated widening the highway that ran through Port Carling.

Good God, was the man crazy?

He'd sold his paper to a redneck conservative. Why broaden the highway unless you wanted more people living in the Port Carling area? And more people would lead to more construction and development.

Hell, Toronto was only three hours away. People didn't need more metropolises. They needed places to escape to. Places like Port Carling, which were just fine the way they were.

Why hadn't he thought to check out this Willard P. Smythe before signing on the dotted line?

It wasn't until Drew flipped to the sports section that his blood really began to boil. Where was Taylor's byline, Warren's pictures? Instead, he found Willard P. Smythe's name beside the coverage of a local softball tournament.

The article itself wasn't bad, and there was nothing wrong with the accompanying photo. But the job of covering the sports desk had meant a lot to those boys and they'd done it well. Too late, Drew realized he should have tried to protect their positions in his contract with Smythe.

He tossed the entire paper into the recycling bin, determined to cancel his subscription. But maybe he'd write a letter to the editor first. He grabbed a notepad and a pen, but paused before the first word.

You gave it up, an inner voice told him. *You moved away. What right do you have to dictate how Smythe runs that paper?*

Drew dropped the notepad. It was only nine. Too early to go to bed. He paced his house restlessly, unable to concentrate on the book he'd been reading or the programs on TV.

The truth was, he was having problems readjusting to life in Ottawa. Starting with that very first night, when he'd unlocked the front door of his house. It hadn't seemed like home; he'd almost felt he was trespassing. The rooms struck him as cold and abandoned, even though he'd arranged for the cleaners to come the day before and freshen things up.

He'd settled in some since then, but he still felt oddly out of place. The problem, of course, was that he hadn't been busy enough. It was going to take some time. He'd been out of circulation for too long. Once word got around, he'd get some meaty stories, and then he'd feel better.

With luck, those stories would require him to

travel to the remote corners of the world, leaving him even less time to think....

Drew paced and paced, and when the phone finally rang, he grabbed it like a lifeline.

"Hello?"

He listened, then smiled and listened some more.

"The Canadian embassy in Washington? You bet I can check out those rumors. How soon do I get started?"

CHAPTER EIGHTEEN

THE ENGINES of the McDonell-Douglas 80 roared on the tarmac at O'Hare airport in Chicago, and Drew tapped his toe impatiently on the briefcase he'd stowed under the seat in front of him.

His broad shoulder was pressed up against the window, and he could barely move his thigh without brushing against the woman beside him. It was so annoying. When he'd flown from Ottawa before this brief stopover in Chicago, the seat beside his aisle one had been vacant. He'd been able to spread his papers, even write out a few notes on his laptop.

But in Chicago a young businesswoman had boarded and claimed the seat next to his. "Could you do me a favor?" she'd asked when he'd stood to let her pass.

"I'm kind of nervous about flying, and looking out the window makes it worse. Would you mind changing seats?"

He would mind. He liked the aisle seat, and he needed the extra room. She could shut the blind, couldn't she? No one was going to force her to look out the window.

But of course he'd said, "Sure," and moved over to the window.

Now she was clutching both arm rests so tightly her hands were visibly shaking.

"I've done a lot of flying and never had any problems," he said.

She nodded tersely. "I'll be okay once we're in the air. Takeoffs are the worst."

Drew glanced at today's copy of the *Globe,* tucked next to his briefcase by his feet, but decided against pulling it out. Reading when the woman beside him was obviously in distress seemed rude. He'd talk to her, try to keep her mind off her fear.

"Are you from Washington?"

She shook her head. She was quite pretty, really, with long wavy brown hair and smooth skin. She was dressed in a pale-blue linen suit and white shirt, and she, too, had a briefcase tucked under the seat in front of her.

"No. I'm from Chicago."

"Going to Washington on business?"

"Yes. My company is hoping to get financing from the International Finance Corporation."

"What business is that?" He wasn't really interested, but he'd noticed her grip on the arm rests had relaxed since they'd started chatting. They spoke a few more minutes, until the seat-belt sign went out.

"Well, we're up," he said. "Excuse me while I grab my briefcase."

"Sure."

Getting his papers out and organized on the small folding tray was a pain. His right elbow kept knocking against the woman, who'd introduced herself as Lydia and was now ordering herself a double scotch.

"Nothing for me, thanks," he said. Where would he put it? He looked at the list of questions he'd been working on and added another.

"Thanks for talking to me," Lydia said. "It helped keep my mind off the takeoff."

Yeah. Well, that was what he'd intended. "No problem," he said. Then he returned his attention to his work. She didn't take the hint, however.

"You didn't tell me anything about yourself. Are you going to Washington on business, too? Your accent sounds Canadian."

"I'm from Port—I mean, I'm from Ottawa," he corrected, covering up the slip quickly. "And yes, I'm in Washington on business, working on story for one of our Canadian newspapers."

"Oh, so you're a journalist." She pressed in toward him, the V neck of her blouse gaping to reveal her cleavage. "How interesting."

There was something very inviting about the way she'd said the word *interesting*. It was the opening move in a game he'd played many times before, but wasn't interested in starting today.

"Yeah, well, it's a job. Excuse me while I—"

She merely peered past his arm. "Are those the questions you're planning to ask?"

"If I get the chance." He flipped over a page, not wanting her to read the exact wording. If the secret source who'd phoned the *Globe* with his suspicions was correct, a major scandal was about to erupt at the Canadian embassy and Drew wanted to be the first to expose it.

"What's the most interesting story you've ever covered?"

He didn't even have to think. "The birth of my daughter. Want to see her picture?" He pulled his wallet out of the breast pocket of his sport jacket and extracted a copy of the hospital photo. "See? Isn't she something?"

"Cute."

"Do you have any kids?" He focused on the pink skin, the tiny pursed mouth. She'd changed a lot since then. He really ought to have a more current picture. He had lots at home, but none of them was wallet size.

"No kids," Lydia said, pulling back from him slightly. "I'm not married."

Me, neither. But he didn't say the words. Instead, he glanced at the photo next to Angel's. It was an old one of him and Mallory, taken on a ski trip to Lake Louise about five years ago. She looked boyish in her ski hat and jacket, but there was no denying the feminine warmth in those mossy eyes or the allure of her soft, peach-colored lips.

In the picture Mallory was laughing, glancing upward slightly to meet his gaze; his arm lay protectively across her shoulders. Drew held the picture closer, trying to remember what they'd been talking about before Grady had sneaked up with the camera.

Probably he'd been teasing her. She had that expression on her face. An ache centered in his heart. He hadn't talked to her in almost a month... somehow it had seemed so hard to pick up the phone.

"Is that your wife?" Lydia asked.

His wife? Drew didn't correct Lydia's natural assumption. The words just wouldn't come, because his mind had disconnected from the present, traveling back in time to that moment with Mallory.

If he tried, he knew he could remember what having her close beside him and laughing had felt like. He stared at the picture, remembering the bite of the wind off the mountain, the thickness of Mallory's braid when he'd tugged it with his gloved hand.

Yes! That was what had happened. He'd pulled her braid and she'd turned to laugh at him, and that was when he'd put his hand over her shoulder. Warmth banished the earlier ache in his heart, and he felt his spirits lift, the way they always did when he was around her.

Always.

Drew went still, then glanced out the window. The blue sky had no discernible beginning or end. Just like his love for Mallory.

Why hadn't he recognized the feeling for what it was years ago?

I love you, Mallory. Had he ever said the words to her the way he was feeling them right now? Intensely, passionately, as if making her believe them was the most important thing in the world. And if he had, would she still have told him to leave?

Cold dread tightened around his chest as he eyed the picture one more time. She might never look at him that way again. By the time he got back to Port Carling she might have found someone else. For sure she'd be so disgusted with how he'd abandoned her and Angel she'd never feel the same about him again.

Oh, God, but he'd blown it.

He slipped the photo back in his wallet and returned the wallet to his jacket. Work beckoned, but for the next twenty minutes, all he could do was stare at his notes. Then the plane began its descent into Washington, D.C.

Lydia was fine as they circled the capital city for landing. Once the plane had taxied to the unloading dock, she stood, smoothing her short skirt over her nicely shaped legs.

"Would you mind getting my bag?"

"Sure." He reached into the overhead compartment and pulled down both of their small suitcases, then followed her off the plane and through the airport. When they reached the main doors, she turned toward him.

"Any chance you'd like to meet for dinner?"

She had pretty lips. Small, full and very kissable. But he shook his head. "I have a lot of work to do. Good luck with the IFC tomorrow."

She gave him a reluctant smile and a wave. "Hope you get back to your family soon."

THE NEXT FEW DAYS WERE CHAOTIC—exactly what Drew had ordered. The story broke after forty-eight hours of intensive investigation, and soon the embassy was swarming with Canadian journalists. Confirmation of the conflict of interest was followed by several resignations. As the reporter who broke the story, Drew found himself being interviewed on TV. And his story was featured on the front of almost all the major Canadian newspapers.

It was all very exciting, but somehow less satisfying than he'd hoped. Where was the adrenaline buzz, the almost heady high he ought to be feeling? A major national news coup was just what he'd longed for when he'd been trapped at the *Gazette*.

Yet it didn't bring him a fraction of the gratification he'd felt helping Terese Balfour turn her life around in Port Carling.

The night before his flight back to Ottawa, Drew stopped by a pub two blocks from his hotel.

The choice of restaurant was no accident. He'd run into someone interesting earlier that day and had made plans to get together over drinks.

Drew pushed through the heavy wooden door into a dark, windowless cavern. It was like stepping back into medieval times, what with the plank flooring and faux-stone walls.

He sat at one of the well-worn bar stools and ordered a beer. While he waited, he played with a package of matches that had been sitting in a nearby ashtray, then pocketed them when the man he'd arranged to meet walked in the door.

The man was in his late fifties at least. Tall and slender, with slightly stooped shoulders and gray hair, he had a weariness about him, as if he'd seen too much of the unsavory side of life.

"David." Drew held up his hand to command his attention.

The older man nodded and headed over. As he climbed onto the stool at Drew's right, he patted the counter in front of him.

"A Boddingtons, sir."

"You bet." The middle-aged bartender snapped the top off a narrow brown bottle and slid it, plus a frosted glass, toward the newcomer.

Drew watched as his companion ignored the glass and tipped the bottle to his lips. He noticed the man's hands—long fingers, well-groomed nails, no wedding ring.

When the man set the bottle down again, it was about a quarter empty. Now Drew focused on his features—the well-spaced blue eyes, a little paler and less focused than when he had met him earlier in the day, and the thin, aristocratic nose.

David Johnstone. He'd been covering the story at the Canadian embassy for the *Washington Post* and had cornered Drew to ask him a few questions.

When he'd introduced himself, Drew couldn't help but make the connection between the man's first name and his age and the description Angie had given him of his father.

Of course there were likely hundreds of journalists named David who lived in the States. Maybe even thousands. But when Drew had asked he'd ever visited Canada, the coincidence became more marked.

"Once," David had said. "When I was just starting out. I couldn't have been much over twenty."

There hadn't been time for more questions, so Drew had offered to buy David Johnstone a beer later. Now Drew tried to sound casual. "So what did you do before working at the *Post?*"

"I taught journalism at a college in Florida for almost twenty-five years. Headed the department for the last five."

"Really?"

"Yeah. Those were good days. My credentials got a little faded, however, and they wanted new blood, so I took early retirement. I thought it would be a better thing than it was. I was never so bored. I decided to move to Washington and try my hand at a little freelance. Then I got an offer from the *Post*...." He slugged back another quarter of the beer and began to pick at the bottle's orange-colored label.

"That's a coincidence," Drew said, ignoring his own beer. "I just went through a career change, too. I sold a paper my grandpa started up in the thirties. The *Hub of the Lakes Gazette*. It's published in Port Carling, a small town in the Muskoka area north of Toronto. Don't imagine you've heard of it?"

Johnstone rubbed the side of his face and sighed. "No. Can't say that I have, although I did spend some time in Toronto when I was younger."

Drew had lifted his glass; now he paused with his beer halfway to his mouth. "I remember you mentioning something about that. When would that have been?"

"Oh, I don't know. Sometime in the early sixties, I guess, back when I was still with the *Miami Herald*. That was where I started my career, and I stayed about four years before I left to work for Associated Press."

The time period was right. The name was right. Hell, everything was right. Drew tapped his fingers on the counter, wondering how to proceed diplomatically. He watched David polish off his beer and then order another.

For sure, he didn't want to scare him off. He could imagine the shock that would etch itself into the lines of the older man's face if he were to ask, *Are you my father?*

No. In this case the direct approach was definitely the wrong approach.

"What story were you working on when you were in Canada?" he asked.

"We were comparing crime statistics in various North American cities. Of course we didn't travel to every city, but Toronto's crime rate was so low— especially compared with Miami's. The editor wanted us to do some digging to find out why."

Drew remembered reading the *Toronto Star* stories on the Internet. They'd been written the winter before he was born. "Did you have your own byline back then?"

"Nah. I was a rookie."

No wonder he'd found no mention of an American reporter named David when he'd searched the Toronto newspapers of that period. Everything fit; everything made sense. Drew gripped his glass of beer tightly and tried to control the buzz of excitement that made it hard to think clearly.

He had no more oblique questions left. The moment had come to plunge to the heart of the matter.

"Did you ever run into a woman named Angie Driscoll? She was my mother and she mentioned meeting an American journalist in December of '62. She spoke very highly of you—I think you made a big impact on her career."

"Yeah? Angie Driscoll?" The name didn't seem to mean anything to David. "I've met a lot of women over the years. Can't say I remember many of them specifically. You know how it is." He shrugged his bony shoulders.

"Sure." Drew stared into the amber liquid in his glass. To feel disappointed was stupid. How had he expected the man to respond? *Oh, yes. Angie Driscoll. I always wondered if she got pregnant after our time together, whether I might actually have a child, a son...*

"You're not married, I take it?"

"Nah. Journalism is one of those careers that doesn't mix well with matrimony, as you must know. You're not married, either, are you?"

Funny. Second time he'd been asked that question. This time, though, he answered it.

"No. I'm not married."

David had pushed off his stool and was now pulling a ten-dollar bill from his pocket.

Drew waved it back at him. "Drinks are on me. Remember?"

"Well, thanks. Sorry I can't stay longer, but I'm meeting a friend for dinner."

He straightened the lapels of his jacket, and Drew could just imagine the sort of friend.

"Nice talking with you, Drew. Maybe we'll see you next time you're in town."

"Yeah. Maybe." With an unwavering gaze, Drew watched the tall man exit the pub.

DREW THOUGHT ABOUT the encounter obsessively later that night, alone in his hotel room. He'd kicked off his shoes, tossed his jacket on a chair, and now he lay sprawled across the double bed, staring unseeingly at music videos on the TV screen.

He'd proven nothing tonight in that short conversation with David Johnstone. All he'd done was identify a possibility.

For the first time in his life, he'd met someone who *could* be his father. The tall American was exactly as Angie had described: a journalist from the States, in town working on a story. And his first name was David.

He *had* to be the man Angie had dated. What were the chances there'd been two American journalists named David in Toronto that winter?

Zilch, Drew was sure.

If only David had remembered Angie...

Drew reflected on the moment he'd said his mother's name; reviewed David's reaction over and over. His conclusion remained the same. Angie's name hadn't meant anything to David—unless, of

course, the man was an excellent actor. But if he
had remembered, why lie? He'd never even known
he'd gotten Angie pregnant, since he'd left town
long before Angie herself had known.

Was this it, then? Was this where Drew's search
ended? With a man who didn't remember his
mother, let alone had any idea he might have conceived a child?

A hollow feeling settled in his gut, and he closed
his eyes. He considered phoning the older journalist.
He could do it right now; he had David's card. Yet
what would he say? *I forgot to mention something
when we met for drinks tonight. I think you're my
father.*

Just the idea brought a laugh. He could imagine
the blank look that would come over David's face.
What the hell are you talking about, boy?

Drew got up and went to the bathroom, shucking
his clothes as he walked. He left his trousers on the
floor, but draped his shirt over the bathroom door-
knob. As he brushed his teeth he gazed at himself
in the mirror, sizing up the similarities between David Johnstone and him. They were both tall, with a
medium complexion and blue eyes. He was willing
to guess that Johnstone's hair had been as dark as
his before it had gone gray.

Beyond that, similarities were hard to spot.

After tossing his toothbrush on the bathroom
counter, Drew rinsed his mouth and then turned off

the light. He sat on the edge of his bed, looking out the window into the street below. What if David Johnstone had been a different sort of man? A warm, sentimental person who'd immediately recognized Angie's name and who'd always wanted a son.

What if he'd been willing to open his heart and his life to the son he'd never known he had?

Was that what Drew had secretly hoped for?

Hell. Angie had already given him the love he'd needed as a child. And, along with his grandpa, she'd taught him the newspaper business backward and forward. It was too late for his dad to teach him to fish; Buddy Conroy had already done that. And Grady's dad had taught him to water-ski.

Drew felt like a damn fool. What exactly had he been spending so much time looking for?

Long moments later, he remembered that he'd taken the letters from Buddy to his mother out of the filing cabinet at work when he'd cleaned out his office at the *Gazette*. They were probably still in his briefcase.

Sure enough, they sat in one of the side pockets. He pulled out the package of matches he'd gotten at the bar and lit the corner of one of the envelopes. The dry paper ignited immediately.

Recalling a scene from a detective series on TV, Drew tossed the envelope into the empty metal trash can, then carried it to the window, which he opened wide so the smoke wouldn't set off the hotel's alarm system.

He threw the remaining envelopes into the trash-can and watched as they quickly collapsed into ash.

So much for the past. It was time to move on to the future.

CHAPTER NINETEEN

"HERE IT IS, DREW," Buddy Conroy said, slapping a contract onto the front desk at the *Gazette*.

"You're a miracle worker, Buddy." Drew picked it up, definitely aware of the irony of the situation. Little more than two months ago Buddy had brought him the agreement to sell his family paper. Now he'd arranged for Drew to buy it back.

"It wasn't that difficult." Buddy sat down opposite Drew. "Smythe's changes to the paper weren't too popular in town. He lost about a dozen subscriptions, and the advertisers were getting right ticked off."

"The dust would have settled."

"Maybe. But Smythe grabbed the chance to back out. He hadn't expected a newspaper to be so much work. He figured he'd be semiretired but he ended up putting in more hours than he had at his job in the city."

"I did warn him."

"I know you did, boy, but it's all worked out in the end, hasn't it? Smythe was able to get his old job back, and his wife was just as happy to return to the city, where their daughter and grandchildren live. Financially you won't lose because I'm waiving my fee.''

"Forget that, Buddy." Drew pulled open a drawer for his checkbook.

"I mean it, Drew. Put that away." Buddy folded his arms over his barrel chest. "I won't cash it, anyway.''

"I appreciate the offer, Buddy. But you don't owe me anything.''

"I don't know about that. You can think of it as a favor to your mother, if you like. Nothing would have meant more to her than having you back in Port Carling, publishing the family paper.''

"Yeah, I'm sure you're right about that," Drew stated running his hands through his thick hair. "If only she were here to see it.''

BUDDY COULDN'T HAVE AGREED with Drew more. Angie should have been alive to see her son return to his hometown. Of his own free will this time. But that was a regret they would both have to live with.

"I just hope you're here for the right reasons.''

Drew glanced around the office, his hands spread out on the desk in front of him. "I think I am, Buddy. I finally realized that I belong here. I feel I can make a difference in this town. And most of all—'' he looked up and met Buddy's gaze "—I want to be here.''

Yes. That was what he'd needed to hear. Buddy relaxed slightly and clasped Drew's shoulder. "I'm glad, Drew. You've been missed."

Most of all by Mallory Lombard, Buddy suspected, but he wasn't sure how much the young woman and her baby had influenced Drew's decision to return, if indeed they had. Well, the child must have been a factor. But what about Mallory?

She'd looked thin and peaked the last time he saw her, and while the pressure of single parenthood could account for some of that, Buddy was pretty sure she'd been missing Drew real bad.

Of course she had. They'd been practically inseparable the months Drew had been home.

Surely Drew had missed her, too. But as a friend? Or as something more?

Oh, Angie. Buddy watched Drew sign the copies of the agreement, then put the papers back in his briefcase.

All these years he'd kept her secret. *Their secret.* He'd never been sure it was right, but she was so certain. And of course he'd had Patricia and his children to consider.

"I won't have my son gossiped about, Buddy Conroy," Angie had said, and that had sealed it.

He'd never breathed a word about the weekend, one month before he'd proposed to Patricia, when he'd driven to Toronto to see if Angie would change her mind about leaving. Her father hadn't had his stroke yet, and she was still determined to have her career. She'd sent Buddy packing, but not before a night of lovemaking that he figured neither one of them had ever forgotten.

No, he hadn't told a soul, except Patricia, who'd decided to marry him anyway. Something he'd always be thankful for. In the end it had worked out fine, even though there'd been a tumultuous couple of months when Angie had returned to town, obviously pregnant, just as he and Patricia were coming back from their honeymoon, Patricia also newly pregnant.

Thanks to Angie's bravery and Patricia's tolerance, everything had sorted itself out in time.

Or had it? Buddy stood up, preparing to leave.

"Thanks again, Buddy," Drew said, shaking his hand.

"Anytime." Buddy exited by the front door, then stopped and turned around. Through the glass window he could see Drew, his attention again focused on the computer monitor on the desk.

Just once, he wished he could tell that boy how proud he was of him. And how much he loved him.

THE RASPBERRIES WERE RED and plump and Mallory had almost picked an ice-cream pail full while Angel slept on a blanket spread over the grass. As she worked she thought of her new neighbors, who'd moved into Drew's house two months ago.

They were an odd couple, strangely antisocial considering they owned the local newspaper. In all the time they'd been here, Mallory hadn't seen Mrs. Smythe leave her house for more than an hour at a time.

Except for today. Mallory had been feeding Angel her cereal this morning when she'd noticed the Smythes climb into their silver Oldsmobile. The strange thing was, Mrs. Smythe had been carrying the plastic kennel they used to transport their cat.

They must have left on a trip.

Now, hearing tires crunching against the graveled laneway, she realized she'd been wrong. They'd just gone for the day. Mallory topped off the pail of berries, thinking she would offer them to the Smythes when they got out of their car.

When she straightened, though, she saw not a silver Oldsmobile but Drew's Explorer.

Impossible.

Yet there he was, stepping out of the driver's side, dressed in jeans and a white button-down shirt. He was looking right at her, and when he saw that she'd spotted him, he smiled.

Stupidly she couldn't think of anything to say. Or maybe the problem was she had too much to say, too many questions to ask.

"I'm guessing you're not exactly pleased to see me." Drew walked through the opening in the hedge; she heard the scratch of the branches as they rubbed against the denim on his legs.

"Why would you say that?"

He'd stopped about five feet away from her. Now he stepped forward, and she wondered if he was going to hug her, but he just plucked the pail out of her hands. Glancing down she saw the ground littered with the berries she'd spent the last half hour picking.

He didn't answer, just bent and started gathering the berries. After a few seconds, she crouched, too, and helped.

"Why didn't you tell me you were coming?" And why hadn't he phoned? In the months he'd been gone, she'd sent several letters, enclosing photos of Angel, but had heard nothing in return. Anger made her want to dump the pail of berries over his head.

"I didn't want to give you a chance to brush me off."

"That's ridiculous."

He picked up the last berry, tucked the full pail back near the hedge, then stood and held out his hand. She ignored it, rising on her own.

"Is it? I've been such an idiot, Mallory. I wouldn't blame you for not wanting to see me."

Suddenly, she wanted to cry. He was Angel's father. She would never keep her baby from him. But, God, how it hurt to see that dear, familiar face again, that lanky, athletic body, and to know that somehow she'd lost the man inside.

"Why are you here, Drew?" Dumb question. To visit Angel, of course.

"I'm moving back."

"To Port Carling?" She was stunned. "Why?"

"Because this is where I want to be."

The words were simple, but there was a look in his eyes... Mallory crossed her arms over her chest and wondered at that expression. It had something soft about it, and warm, and just a little possessive. It reminded her of the way he'd looked at Angel when she was born; only, he was looking at *her* this time, and there was a glint in his eyes that was definitely not fatherly.

"I'm home for good, Mallory. I've bought back the paper and Smythe and his wife are returning to Toronto."

Mallory took a gulp of air. She couldn't believe—"Well, that explains the cat carrier."

"What? No, never mind." He took another step toward her. "I've been waiting a long time to tell you something. Something I couldn't do over the phone or in a letter."

Panic made her hold her breath.

"I love you, Mallory. I've always loved you."

It wasn't what she'd expected. She'd given up hoping. These past few months she'd reconciled herself to losing his friendship as well as the chance for a future together. Now, all of a sudden, it was all too much. She couldn't help it: she burst into tears.

"Sweetheart." Drew sounded alarmed. He gathered her in his arms. "Don't you believe me? Or can't you forgive me for hurting you so badly? Or is there someone—?"

"Oh, hush." Finally, she could get a few words out. She cupped the sides of his face with her hands and locked her gaze with his. "When you say you love me, what kind of love are you talking about?"

She had to ask the question, even though she was sure she could see the answer in his eyes. Drew had never looked at any of his old girlfriends like this. She'd never seen him look at *anyone* like this.

"The true-love kind," he said. "The Humphrey Bogart and Ingrid Bergman kind."

She pulled back. "They don't end up together at the end of *Casablanca,* you know."

He grimaced, then cast his eyes around for a moment. "Okay, the Meg Ryan and Tom Hanks kind."

"That's better." Meg and Tom *always* ended up together. "Now, kiss me, Drew. Kiss me and convince me that you mean it."

He did, and the kiss was the sweetest of her life. Sweeter than a dish—no, a pail—of raspberries. She clung to his neck, not sure she could believe he was really here, that his mouth was covering hers, that his arms were tight around her.

"Mallory, Mallory."

She was trembling and he was stroking her arms. She watched him through a sheen of tears, and felt how tenderly he brushed his hand along her hair, then her face and her lips.

It was true. He was here.

Drew.

And he was finally hers.

THERE WAS A LITTLE SQUAWK from somewhere on the ground, followed by the beginning of a cry.

Drew turned to see his daughter on a blanket in the shade of the old maple.

"Hello, precious." He looked down at Angel, and his heart felt as if it had doubled in size in that one moment. She'd changed, become prettier, he thought, and her hair was definitely growing in blond.

"Isn't she adorable?"

Mallory was steadier now. She'd stopped crying, and her color was returning to normal. She'd appeared so pale when she'd first seen him he'd been terrified that he was too late—that he truly had blown his chances with her. Now he slipped his arms from around her and reached for his baby.

"Angel…" Thank God she didn't make strange. He noticed, though, that her eyes followed Mallory's every movement. He tucked her up against his shoulder and put his other arm around Mallory's waist. She leaned in against him and for a few minutes they just stood, observing their daughter as she yawned and stretched after her nap.

"Why, Drew?" Mallory asked suddenly, pulling back from him a little. "Why did you come back? And why now?"

Drew thought of that moment on the plane when he'd realized how completely he loved her. How to explain something like that?

"Was it Smythe's editorials?"

"Yeah. They really sucked." He tightened his arm around her. "Plus, I missed my best friend. I had no one to talk to in Ottawa, no one to tease and no one to watch those sappy videos with. You ever have a friend like that?"

Her bottom lip quivered as she held out her right hand, then her left. "Best friends for life," she said quietly.

"And so much more," he added, lowering his head to whisper in her ear. "Lover, and mother of my child, and woman I want to spend the rest of my life with. Please believe me, Mallory. And tell me you'll marry me this time."

She wasn't quite convinced. He could tell by the way her gaze drifted down to rest on Angel's face. "I read your articles on the Canadian embassy scandal," she said. "Major front-page news. That must have made you so happy."

"I haven't felt a moment's happiness since I left.

You don't believe me, do you? What if I told you that even if you turn me down, I'm not going anywhere." He looked at the child in his arms. He was going to be here for her. As much as Mallory would let him.

"I met a man when I was in Washington on assignment. I'm pretty sure he was my father—he sounded just like the man Angie said she dated that last year of college."

"Oh, Drew. Did he remember Angie?"

"No. At first I was really disappointed, then I saw it didn't matter. Whether he was my biological father or not, he was still a stranger. The people who are important are here, always have been. Why search for something you already have?"

A loud, obnoxious sound, followed rapidly by a foul smell, came from the bundle in his arms.

"Oh, great. My daughter is now interrupting my soliloquies with her bowel movements."

Mallory laughed. "Get used to it, Drew. You're going to be experiencing a lot of it. And you better change her fast. Her skin is really sensitive."

"Not until you tell me you love me at least half as much as I love you. Not until you promise you'll marry me as soon as possible. Not until—" he paused as she began to push him in the direction of the house "—you tell me where the baby wipes are."

"I'll do better than tell you. I'll show you."

"Where the baby wipes are?"

"Yes. And then how much I love you."

"Do you mean that, Mallory?" He reached out with his one free hand and pulled her close for a kiss. She tasted like raspberries, and her hair smelled like summer meadows. He felt the aching in his groin at the same moment as her firm breasts pressed against his chest.

"I love you, Drew. Never doubt it."

Once in the house, she gave him a push toward the bathroom. "Change that diaper and come out here and I'll prove it."

"With pleasure." He set Angel on the plastic pad that was spread out on the bathroom counter and unsnapped her sleepers. Tearing back the tabs on the diaper, he saw the extent of the damage.

Whew! He was definitely going to need those baby wipes.

CHAPTER TWENTY

THE DRESS HAD ARRIVED with a late spring shipment, and Mallory had set it aside without being honest about her intentions.

"This is too fancy for Port Carling," she'd said. "No sense even putting it on the rack."

The truth was, it would make a perfect wedding dress, although she hadn't dared even to think such a thought back then, not with Drew acting so strange.

Now, three months later, Mallory swiveled in front of the full-length mirror in her bedroom and watched the creamy silk fabric dance around her lower legs. The dress was absolute simplicity, with long sleeves and a scoop-necked bodice, designed to follow the contours of her waist and hips, before spilling out into a generous skirt that fell to her lower calves.

"It's perfect on you," Terese said. "Come here and let me fix your hair."

She'd already applied Mallory's makeup. Now she French-braided the hair on the sides of her head, leaving the back long. "Let's put on some spray conditioner so it isn't quite so wild.'' She gave a few squirts with a bottle from Claire's seemingly bottomless beauty-supplies kit.

"How about some baby's breath in her braids?" Claire suggested. She was holding Angel on one hip; a flannel blanket covered her shoulder to protect her pale-pink sheath.

"Good idea." Terese picked a few strands from the bouquet.

Baby's breath. Mallory's gaze settled lovingly on her daughter, who was now almost five months old, and thought you couldn't get any more appropriate than that.

"There." Terese stood back and examined her handiwork. "I think she's ready. What do you say, Claire?"

"Definitely."

Mallory held out her hands to them. "I'm so glad you're here. Both of you. I still can't believe this is really happening."

In forty minutes she would to be standing in front of family and friends, promising her love and devotion to the man she'd once considered her best friend and now thought of as so much more.

When had that friendship turned to love? There was no simple answer. It had been a gradual thing, so gradual that they might have missed it if not for Angel and the miracle of her life.

She would have to thank her daughter for that,

maybe on Angel's wedding day. Mallory took a last glance in the mirror, then picked up her bouquet. She was definitely ready.

BUDDY CONROY SAT holding his wife's hand in his lap. He'd always liked weddings. Listening to joyful couples making their vows reminded him of the potential of marriage, a potential that all too few people took full advantage of, in his opinion.

Mallory, glowing with love and happiness, was a bride who truly touched the heart. And Drew was dashingly handsome, with eyes only for his bride. Buddy knew Angie would have been delighted with this marriage. As was he.

Listening to Mallory promise her friendship, devotion and love, Buddy squeezed Patricia's hand. He'd had all those from his wife, and hoped he'd given as much as he'd received. She squeezed back and smiled, tiny wrinkles fanning out from the corners of her eyes. Those wrinkles hadn't been there thirty-five years ago, but they hadn't known as much about love and pain and compromise in those days, either.

Suddenly, Mallory and Drew were kissing, and organ music was pumping through the church.

"Don't they make a darling couple?" Patricia put her lips next to his ear to say. "Mallory is positively radiant."

"The most beautiful woman in the room," he agreed. "Next to you."

IT WAS ONE OF THOSE MOMENTS that Mallory always treasured. Her closest friends gathered together, this time to celebrate her wedding to Drew. Claire and Kirk had volunteered their spacious cottage for the reception, although Mallory had insisted the buffet dinner be catered.

"You will not spend my wedding in the kitchen," she'd stated.

"No. I'll spend it baby-sitting your daughter." Then Claire had laughed, because there was no shortage of volunteers when it came to attending to the adorable baby.

Right now, Kirk was holding her, and all three of his girls were taking turns making her smile. As Mallory watched, Claire came up from behind and put a hand on Kirk's shoulder. He turned and smiled at her.

The perfect family. Even as she thought it, Mallory knew she was oversimplifying. There was no such thing as a perfect family, and Claire and Kirk had their own special challenges to overcome. She was just thankful that they seemed to be doing exactly that.

"I hate to say this," Drew said from behind her as he wrapped his hands around her waist, "but your hair is incredibly beautiful today."

"Thanks to Terese." Mallory leaned back into her husband. "Look around, Drew. Everyone who means something to us is here." Even her aunt Norma, although unable to attend on such short notice, had managed to send a telegram, with assurances of a wedding gift to follow by post.

Drew tucked his head in beside hers. "And look at Terese. She and Lisa fit in so well you'd think they'd grown up here like the rest of us."

The petite, dark-haired beauty was chatting with the Conroys, while her daughter played with a couple of the children she knew from day care.

"I'm so glad they've settled here. I think Terese will do some wonderful painting once she sets her mind to it."

"And there's Grady, standing by the fireplace. Doesn't he look sad?"

"Yes, he does, Drew. It makes me feel awful. Imagine what he's going through, attending our wedding when his own marriage has broken up."

Bess was someone who should have been here but wasn't. A sign that the world was not quite as ideal as Mallory would wish it.

"I'll go talk to him," Drew said. But before he'd even removed his hands from Mallory's waist, they saw Claire walk up to him and put her hand on his shoulder.

"I hope he'll be okay."

"He will," Drew said. "He has his friends, and he has his boys."

The twins had been crawling all over Drew just minutes earlier. Mallory had begun to wonder if she'd get a minute with her new husband all night. They'd been ushers for the wedding, and of course they'd had their jobs with the *Gazette* reinstated.

"If only Angie were here, the day would be perfect."

Mallory turned and took his hands in hers. "That's exactly what I was thinking."

"Although I do wonder if we'd be here right now if she hadn't died. It's awful to say, but I think it took her death to shock me into making some decisions about the kind of life I was leading and the kind of man I wanted to be."

Mallory leaned in closer, pressing her cheek against his starched white shirt. "And what kind of man do you want to be?"

"The kind whose mother could come to him if she was sick and know she could depend on him."

"Oh, Drew…"

"Don't worry, Mal. I don't say that out of bitterness. I know Angie loved me and she knew I loved her, too. But reliability wasn't my long suit. You know that better than most."

"Maybe so, Drew. But I still think you're being hard on yourself. Angie just wanted to protect you for as long as she could. She thought she had more time...."

"What a year," Drew reflected. "A death, a birth and now a marriage."

"It's like my aunt Norma always said, I guess."

"Aunt Norma?"

Mallory patted down a tuft of Drew's hair that was sticking out at an odd angle. At the same moment he reached for a strand of her hair that had escaped the braid.

"Sure," Mallory said. "Aunt Norma. She was always saying, *Just goes to show, you never can tell.*"

Wasn't it the truth.

* * *

Look for Claire's story, The Fourth Child, *coming in April.*

▼ SILHOUETTE®
SUPERROMANCE™

AVAILABLE FROM 18TH JANUARY 2002

THE PULL OF THE MOON Darlene Graham

9 Months Later

Dr Danni Goodlove would like to blame everything on the moon—Matt's crazy proposal, her equally crazy acceptance and the unusual marriage ceremony—followed by her new husband's tender lovemaking. Now, just as Danni's regaining her senses, she's having a baby….

DR DAD Judith Arnold

Toby Cole is sure Susannah Dawson will be a positive influence in his daughter, Lindsey's, life. Lindsey loves Susannah and before long Toby and Susannah have to admit that they've fallen in love, too. It sounds ideal. *It's not!* But it could be…

THE BABY BET: HIS SECRET SON
Joan Elliott Pickart

The Baby Bet

Kara MacAllister had dedicated her life to earning the respect and love of the MacAllisters. Now a stranger was threatening everything she held dear. Yet even knowing that, she couldn't stop her attraction to the man Andrew Malone had shown her he could be. All she could do was trust him.

THE REAL FATHER Kathleen O'Brien

Twins

Molly Lorring left home pregnant with Beau Forrest's baby. But no one would ever know because Beau had died not knowing he was to be a father. Except Beau's identical twin, Jackson, carried his own secret—Beau *wasn't* the father of Molly's baby…

2 FREE

books and a surprise gift!

We would like to take this opportunity to thank you for reading this Silhouette® book by offering you the chance to take TWO more specially selected titles from the Superromance™ series absolutely FREE! We're also making this offer to introduce you to the benefits of the Reader Service™—

★ FREE home delivery
★ FREE gifts and competitions
★ FREE monthly Newsletter
★ Exclusive Reader Service discount
★ Books available before they're in the shops

Accepting these FREE books and gift places you under no obligation to buy, you may cancel at any time, even after receiving your free shipment. Simply complete your details below and return the entire page to the address below. *You don't even need a stamp!*

YES! Please send me 2 free Superromance books and a surprise gift. I understand that unless you hear from me, I will receive 4 superb new titles every month for just £3.49 each, postage and packing free. I am under no obligation to purchase any books and may cancel my subscription at any time. The free books and gift will be mine to keep in any case.

U2ZEA

Ms/Mrs/Miss/Mr ....Initials.....................................
BLOCK CAPITALS PLEASE

Surname ....

Address ....

....

....Postcode...................................

Send this whole page to:
UK: FREEPOST CN81, Croydon, CR9 3WZ
EIRE: PO Box 4546, Kilcock, County Kildare (stamp required)